"You aren

Marie's hand moved toward her gun.

"I'd recommend you leave that gun where it is if you want to live," the deputy said. "Right now, we're friends, but that can change."

In the rearview mirror, Marie saw a man's silhouette in the light. He walked toward the passenger side.

"Turn your truck off and throw your keys onto the ground. Keep your hands where I can see them."

Marie did as the deputy ordered.

"Do you see damage on that side of the vehicle?" the deputy asked.

"No, but it would be primarily up front."

In the headlights, Marie saw the man's dark hair and haunting blue eyes. Wade Trapper was taller and more handsome than his picture.

It was a wonder he could blend in when working overseas. He had to stick out.

Yet people often said the same about her. Like her, he must have made it work.

Or, in his case, a little too well.

It was up to her to discover his alliances.

MURDER IN THE MOUNTAINS

DANICA WINTERS

Recycling programs for this product may not exist in your area.

ISBN-13: 978-1-335-08247-3

Murder in the Mountains

For questions and comments about the quality of this book, please contact us at CustomerService@Harlequin.com.

TM and ® are trademarks of Harlequin Enterprises ULC.

Harlequin Enterprises ULC
22 Adelaide St. West, 41st Floor
Toronto, Ontario M5H 4E3, Canada
www.Harlequin.com

HarperCollins Publishers
Macken House, 39/40 Mayor Street Upper,
Dublin 1, D01 C9W8, Ireland
www.HarperCollins.com

Printed in U.S.A.

Danica Winters is a multiple-award-winning, bestselling author who writes books that grip readers with their ability to drive emotion through suspense and occasionally a touch of magic. When she's not working, she can be found in the wilds of Montana, testing her patience while she tries to hone her skills at various crafts—quilting, pottery and painting are not her areas of expertise. She believes the cup is neither half full nor half empty, but it better be filled with wine. Visit her website at danicawinters.net.

Books by Danica Winters

Harlequin Intrigue

West Glacier Ranch Suspense

Rodeo Crime Ring
Mystery on the Range
Stalked in the Mountains
Murder in the Mountains

Big Sky Search and Rescue

Helicopter Rescue
Swiftwater Enemies
Mountain Abduction
Winter Warning

STEALTH: Shadow Team

A Loaded Question
Rescue Mission: Secret Child
A Judge's Secrets
K-9 Recovery
Lone Wolf Bounty Hunter
Montana Wilderness Pursuit

Visit the Author Profile page at Harlequin.com.

CAST OF CHARACTERS

Wade Trapper—The main protagonist, described as the sexiest of the Trapper siblings, who has returned home with deep emotional scars from his military service. He is under investigation by the CIA for his involvement in the deaths of his teammates.

Marie Costa—A neurodivergent military contractor sent by the CIA to investigate Wade. She is intelligent and direct, bringing a unique perspective to the story.

Emily Trapper—Wade's sister-in-law, she plays a crucial role in bridging the gap between him and Marie.

Kim Gonzalez—The director's right-hand assistant, a woman who seems to know all the secrets.

Rick Anciaux—The director of Rogue Warrior and a man who seems to believe he is the center of the world.

Shawn Lichten—Wade's teammate from the Vaquero Group who is the head of tech, a man who is not without flaws.

Prologue

It was common knowledge to never trust the safety on any weapon. A black knob, lever, or switch, it didn't matter—once clicked to the red, all one had to do was place the tip of the finger on the trigger, give a smooth exhale, and slowly pull.

An enemy would be vanquished. Life extinguished.

People could be saved.

Battles might be won.

Unfortunately, the wars Wade Trapper now faced were not that easy to win. A trigger pull would only exacerbate the problems in his life and draw him further into the horror of his past and the false reality of the future.

Dissociation was his only solace.

Mark, Andrew, Shawn, and James sat beside him in the burrow pit as he held the M4 against his chest. He gripped it like it was some kind of religious icon in hopes that it could save his soul, but in a sandy abyss where time became endless, his only constant and reliable company was his own breath. Even that relationship was tenuous. Many of his fellow teammates from the Vaquero Group had lost the battle for more.

Nathen, Anton, and Jason had just lost theirs.

The smoke from their burning Escalade curled up into the sky, marking their last moments and harkening what was just around the corner for the rest of their team.

The missile had missed them, but the bomb had struck with deadly accuracy. They had barely made it out of the SUV before the explosion.

Now he and the others were on their own to escape this cancerous city.

Their drones buzzed overhead, and he could hear them bugging out from the hit they had just made on their team on the road. It was a nation like every other country he'd been hired to work in over the last six years. Each day bled into the next until there were days like this, where his blood was the next set to spill.

Their enemy combatants were now just outside of his sight line, but they were hunkered down on the top of the stucco building just to the south. James gave him the thumbs-up and pointed at the portable screen he used to control and see from the drones.

Wade gave him a nod. This was their only way out.

There was an unmistakable whistle as the bomb dropped and careened into its assigned coordinates. He didn't bother to cover his ears; it didn't matter. The percussion moved through his body, hitting with the force of an invisible wave. He would hurt in more ways than one tomorrow.

Smoke filled the air. It smelled of dust, burnt rubber, oil, and fats.

It didn't bother him. If anything, it was the smell of revenge.

A life stolen was not to be ignored. Not when it came to commitment, brotherhood, and fealty to the greater good.

Mark jabbed his elbow hard into his side and motioned southward. "Those birds are rolling hot. Gonna hit 59 on the 86," he said with his slight British accent.

He gripped his assault rifle tighter, his lifeline in this living nightmare. "Let them pop smoke and drop vengeance. Our brothers watch."

It was strange, this juxtaposition between reverence for their friends whom they had lost and the derision for the faceless living.

Mark gave him a fist bump. “Brothers.”

James followed suit.

The wind picked up and carried the scent of battle. He both loved and hated that smell, as in it was the promise of a short and brutal future. Today was for living, tomorrow was forgotten, and safety could only be found on a gun.

Chapter One

Montana had sung to him like a Greek Siren—her wings were the rainbows cast by the sunset, her beauty the blue crystal waters of Flathead Lake mirrored by the sky, and her talons the sharp Mission Mountains. Wade had known the dangers of succumbing to her cries. To yield to her was to be lured to the rocks of his past which would likely be his end. Yet for him, the call home was inescapable.

Stepping off the plane and onto Montana soil, the song of his Siren hit its climax, an aria of ghosts and promises.

Death was his everything, but Montana was his home. If he was to die, it would be where he had been born and not on the sands of a foreign nation he could not name or admit having entered.

Here, his Siren could have him, and he would be faceless no longer.

If anything, she would be the proof he needed to ensure he still held a soul.

His brother, Cameron Trapper, was standing in the lobby of the Missoula airport. The place was totally unlike the airport it had been when he'd left six years ago. Then it looked like his grandfather's living room from the 1970s, complete with orange tiles and faded brown walls. Now the place looked like many other modern airports, complete with the required coffee shop and bar.

Cameron had his head down, working away on his phone. He tapped quickly, too busy to notice Wade, and he thought about seizing the moment to go have one more beer before facing this new, and somehow old, reality.

If someone had told him he would be settling back down in his former home instead of becoming just another casualty of secret wars, he wouldn't have believed them. Hell, even now, he barely trusted the moment.

He doubted he deserved this, but it was the only place he had wanted to be after he had taken his latest contract. He needed a break from his warped reality and somewhere that reminded him of easier times, when he could still feel human.

Before he walked out the exit and into the

main lobby, Wade weaved to the bathroom. He splashed water onto his face, as if in doing so, he could wash away any clear evidence on his face that would allow his brother to guess at the horrors of all he had experienced.

Looking at the crow's feet at the corners of his eyes, he knew he couldn't hide the ravages of living nightmares from prematurely aging him.

He forced a smile in the mirror—the expression was so foreign to him that he didn't recognize himself. He wasn't bad looking, but it was a good thing he wasn't looking to find a woman. His searches would have come up dry.

"She must be a looker." A man walked up from behind him and started to wash his hands. "Take it from me—just go for it. Don't let anything stand in your way when it comes to love. Life is too short for accepting anything short of amazing."

His smile must have done its job, or the man was just horrible at reading body language. Regardless, the stranger couldn't have been more wrong. The last thing he was looking for in Montana was love, and if he did somehow trip into something even minorly resembling a relationship, he would be the first one to get back onto a plane.

He would be doing womankind a favor in never wanting anything more than a good time, and the world a favor if he never had kids. Even the *good time* part was something that was so far in his distant past that if pressed to remember, it had been a date that ended with a hug on his prom date's doorstep at the end of the night. Not that he would ever admit that to the guys in the forward operating base, or FOB.

As far as any of his teammates were concerned, he wasn't to be left alone with a beautiful woman or she wouldn't be able to help herself—in fact, a couple of his former teammates had dubbed him "Lover Boy." Oh, the irony.

He looked at the guy washing his hands at the sink next to him. "Thanks, man. 'Preciate the advice." He dried his hands and walked out, not wanting to hear another word from the well-meaning dude.

His footfalls echoed out in the almost empty lobby, washing over the sound of distant voices coming from the small baggage claim area. Cameron looked up with the noise, and there was an unexpected darkness on his face that made Wade regret having bothered to practice his false felicity.

"If I thought you were going to greet me like that, I could've gotten a taxi," Wade said with a forced laugh, nervous that he had made a mistake in coming to this place if that was how his brother truly felt about his being there.

Cameron had told him he was welcome, that they were expanding the ranch, and that if he could find respite there as long as he needed before heading back to the United States secret battles.

His brother was just as bad at fake smiles as he was, and his mouth pulled into a misaligned arc that didn't even remotely speak of joy. "Sorry. Not you. Just dealing with things at the ranch."

A sense of relief passed over him, but he pulled the bag on his shoulder higher like it was some metaphorical weight from the past and with each step closer to the ranch it was growing immeasurably heavier.

"I bet you've got your hands full all the time now, boss man." He slapped his brother on the shoulder jovially. "I'm shocked that the place is still up and running with you in charge," he joked, though he was more than well aware the place had only survived thanks to Cameron and his siblings' ongoing efforts.

"Trust me, brother, some days that makes

two of us." Cameron ran his hand through his shaggy hair and sent him a tired look. "This job can take it out of a guy. Then again, I'm sure I can't complain about anything compared to you, you big world traveler."

The weight on his shoulders grew heavier. "Ah, all I do is ingratiate myself with locals," he said, carefully sidestepping around the truths of his employment and its realities. There were some parts of his life that no one here needed to know. As far as his family was concerned, they knew he did work for the government but nothing about his job's particulars.

They walked out into the fall afternoon. The air was hazy with wildfire smoke, and there was a thin layer of gray ash on his brother's ranch truck. He tossed his bag into the back seat and climbed in. His brother kicked on the pickup, and as the AC turned on it carried the stale scent of wet ash. The smell drew him back into that last moment in the desert, when the drones had been buzzing overhead.

Even with the air conditioning, a heavy sweat started to form on his skin, and he was forced to push away a droplet that twisted down his temple, moving through the stubble on his cheeks.

"You feeling okay?" his brother asked, driving out of the lot and stopping at the toll booth and handing over his ticket. A white Toyota Tacoma pulled into the lane behind them, a woman behind the wheel. "You're looking a little pale. We can stop at Bojangles and get you some food if you're hungry or whatever. You know they've got the best chicken-fried steak around."

He loved that his brother's answer to his discomfort was food. Not the healthiest option, true, but at least he didn't really want to talk about it—just acknowledge the issue and cover it up with some greasy hash browns and gravy. That was his kind of therapy.

"Sounds good," he said. He hadn't eaten a good brown American meal in six months, and the last thing he'd eaten of substance had been bread pudding right before he'd caught his flight out of Cairo, which had been hours ago.

For the next couple of hours, they made small talk and caught up about Cameron's new wife and their siblings, but they both carefully avoided the topic of what their father had done to put Cameron in the role as ranch owner. It made him feel a touch better knowing that his brother had a few unwelcome conversations in his world as well. Guarded was the only way to be, not only in contracting but in ranching, too. If not, they both had a rawness that could wear on a person.

The restaurant hadn't changed the slightest since he had been there the last time, when he had been a kid, complete with blue vinyl booths along the walls and chrome swiveling bar stools at its center. There was a train that chugged around the tracks overhead, and the place smelled like old fryer grease and decades of Aqua Netted servers. A woman in her late sixties scooted by carrying a tray of coffee cups and a carafe, and though he couldn't be completely sure, he could have sworn it was the original server.

She turned back and gave him an appraising look. "If it isn't Wade Trapper," she said, with a wide smile. "Welcome home, kiddo. You and Cam take seats anywhere you'd like. I'll be right with ya." She lifted her tray a bit higher as a testament that she would have helped them right then and there had it not been for the five pounds of items already in her care.

He couldn't have named the woman if someone had paid him, but he attempted to return the smile as best he could even though his cheeks were aching. "Thank you, ma'am."

He sent Cam a look, and his brother winked in response. News of his coming home must have traveled fast in the town—that or his brother spent entirely too much time at the place. Either way, he'd spent so long not being seen that it made his skin prickle.

The door jingled behind him, and as he turned, he saw the white Tacoma with the same woman from the airport in the driver's seat. She looked at him with a wicked smile as she gripped the wheel, and the truck careened toward the front of the building.

The wave of sound hit him with the percussive blast, blowing him back, but he threw his body toward his brother in hopes of blocking him from the explosion. The world blurred and dust filled the air. In the distance, there was the reminiscent whirring sound like that of drones, the sounds of his nightmares.

Chapter Two

The phone call stirred Marie Costa from the best hour of sleep she'd experienced ever since she had landed in Seattle. The damp gray skies bore down on her as she wrestled with the buzzing phone, trying to push away the dregs of drowsiness that threatened to slur her words like drunkenness. No one needed to see her as anything less than a well-oiled machine.

According to the screen, it was a private number calling, which meant only one thing—she was being called to work.

She should have known that this vacation was a farce. There really was no rest for the weary. If she was lucky, her bosses within the Falcon Group would only be sending her somewhere that would include only a stop in London and not three jumps and a bumpy two-bit Duct taped truck into the heart of a FOB in a nameless country. She'd had enough of that for the year.

So far, she'd been in thirteen countries on four continents. Pressed, she wasn't sure she could name them all, nor could she say she cared to—her job as a military contracting lead operative had been completed to the best of her abilities at each, there was no looking back and no room for armchair quarterbacking after the fact.

The thought made the looming Seattle rain clouds overhead look less ominous and more like weighted blankets and, oddly, it brought her comfort. As much as she didn't want to be called off of her much-deserved vacation, she loved her job, and she loved the gray. Everything about her was one click off normal and it always had been. While the other girls were reveling in the pomp and extravagance of the prom, she was making her dress out of Starburst wrappers, only the red ones.

There had been whispers about her being neurodivergent because of her ability to always feel more comfortable with animals in any situation and her penchant to spew odd facts whenever she felt the need to fill an uncomfortable silence. She'd never been tested, she didn't care what others thought of her, or where she lay on someone's spectrum. She was who she was, and the people who she worked for now seemed to think she fit the bill.

She would never lose her love for all things animals—and she'd made it clear the day she'd been brought on as a contractor that it would be her weak point. Her boss, Corey Trixi, had assured her that her weakness was one of the most common in the field—and especially for Americans.

Her phone buzzed again, and she answered. "Yes?"

"You up to a run?" She recognized Corey's voice.

"Anything you need. Just send me the info."

"It should be a short one, just a half marathon. Near the Canadian border."

"No problem."

The line went dead, and she appreciated the clear, no-nonsense ending. It was one of her favorite qualities about Corey, he was like her in his ability to cut to the chase. Give what needed to be given, go. Simple.

And that was probably why she had never had a functional or healthy romantic relationship in her entire life. Every man she had dated had told her she was cold and uncommunicative. She would definitely give them the uncommunicative part, but with her job, there wasn't much she could have told them about her daily life. Some had understood, but whatever cool factor her job carried to help them to empathize had quickly worn off and was replaced by annoyance and resentment.

The encrypted email popped up on her computer on the hotel's desk. Opening up the email, she couldn't believe what she was reading—she was headed to Montana. A truck was waiting.

She had never operated inside the states before. It wasn't unheard of, but it was uncommon as they typically worked under only the laws set forth by the United Nations—and sometimes even those were a little fuzzy.

IT TOOK MARIE COSTA ten hours to reach the coordinates Corey had sent her—it would have taken her nine hours and forty-seven minutes if she hadn't had to stop for gas, but apparently whomever had set up her Tacoma hadn't thought she needed a full tank. They would be hearing from her later.

Epic fail.

They wouldn't be a part of her background team again, or she wouldn't be taking the next assignment. Corey knew better than to skip steps—it was the difference between life and death.

She had been sent here to get eyes on one Wade Trapper, a possible double agent. He'd left his group under questionable circumstances and a series of his teammates had died while working to protect a gold shipment that had then gone missing. There was talk that he had even pulled the trigger and the bullion was in his hands.

It was dark when she arrived outside the West Glacier Ranch. There were floodlights set up outside the red barn and from where she had parked on the side of the highway in front of the location to scope, it appeared as though there was some kind of filming taking place. A man clad in a blue suit with a red tie standing on a podium, a red, white and blue flag pinned to the front and he was wagging his fist like a politician making a rallying speech.

The last thing she needed to happen was for her to be caught on camera, so she kicked her truck into gear and sped off into the darkness.

As she rounded the bend in the road, heading toward the next assigned hotel, her mirror lit up with red and blue flashing lights. She gut checked and glanced down at her speedometer, she hadn't been speeding.

She rolled her right foot, feeling the bump of the pistol strapped inside her boot. There was another on her hip. If someone had set her up with this cop, they had better be ready. They were foolish if they thought she was going to go down without a fight.

Pulling the car over to the side of the road, she flipped down the visor like she was just a normal chick and started to check her makeup and hair. The game was on. The sheriff's deputy was wearing a hat tilted low down on their forehead, reminding her of a highway patrolman. Their blinding light was glaring into the rearview mirror.

The deputy tapped on the driver's side window with their flashlight and then shined it into her car. She rolled down her window and plastered the most coquettish smile she could muster across her face. The woman looked up from under her hat. "You aren't from around here, are you?" the deputy asked.

Her hand moved slightly as she went for the Sig Sauer on her hip.

"I'd strongly recommend you leave that gun exactly where it is if you want to live," the deputy said. "Right now, we are friends, but that can quickly change." She motioned toward her car.

Looking into the rearview mirror, Marie could see the silhouette of a V-shaped man's torso in the light behind her. The guy walked toward the passenger side.

"I want you to turn your truck off and throw your keys onto the ground outside the door," the deputy ordered. "Keep your hands where I can see them."

Things were going sideways, but she didn't know why. She couldn't get arrested. If this was something minor, she dang sure couldn't get caught up in some small-town line up for something she had no business being rounded up in. And if this was tied to her work as a contractor, she couldn't allow herself to fall into enemy hands—she would kill long before she would allow herself to be killed.

She turned off the truck with the push of a button, and picked up the keys from the console and, instead of throwing them on the ground outside the truck, she put them on the roof. The deputy scowled, but didn't make her move them.

"Do you see any damage on that side of the vehicle?" the deputy asked.

"No, but it would be primarily up front."

The man walked around to the front of her pickup and in the light, she saw the man's dark hair and haunting blue eyes.

As he moved between the shadows and the lights, Wade Trapper appeared like a ghost rising from the dust. He was far more handsome than he was in the pictures she had been sent in the email this morning. And she had known he was tall, but he looked even more impressive at 6'3" in real life.

It was a wonder how he could have blended in when working overseas as a contractor, especially in countries where some of the men's average heights were only in the high five-foot range. He had to stick out.

Yet, people often said the same things about her and her sex. It wasn't easy being a woman in her chosen profession. Just like her, he must have made it work.

Or, in his case, a little too well.

It was up to her to discover his alliances.

Chapter Three

The woman was undeniably beautiful. The kind of pretty that came without trying but also screamed for a man to proceed with caution. She likely had her choice in guys and from the way she looked at him, found them to be a nuisance.

Her blond hair was tied back into a tight no nonsense braid that his sister Jamie used to only wear when she was going to work with horses. It was the hairstyle of a woman who didn't want to be bothered, and it made him wondered if she ever let it down. If she had, it probably would have been well past her breasts.

As she stepped out of her truck, he noticed that the left was slightly smaller than the right and he couldn't quite put his finger on it, but he found a bit of comfort in the fact that she wasn't totally one-hundred-percent perfect. If she had been, he wouldn't have even thought about her as a potential bed mate.

Not that he was thinking about her in that way. No.

Especially not here, standing on the side of the highway in front of the ranch in the middle of the night, while he and his sister-in-law Emily Trapper were trying to stand watch in hopes of stopping any more attacks from raining down on him or his family. They couldn't risk losing the filming contracts that were pouring money into the ranch and keeping them not only afloat, but ahead for several years to come.

According to his brother Cameron, it was a first and it was all because the family had finally come together in one cohesive unit. Wade couldn't be the one to come barreling in and screwing it all up. If anything, if the attack at the diner proved to be anything other than a mistake or a one-off, then he would need to hit the road. It didn't matter how much he wanted to be home, he couldn't put his family at risk.

His brother had found a winner with Emily, and standing there watching her work over the beautiful blonde who had done nothing more than make a mistake by stopping to rubberneck on the side of a highway, he was impressed. He could see why his brother had chosen Emily; they were cut from the same cloth. It made him wish for a passing moment that he had followed in his brother's footsteps instead of running away to the world's most dangerous destinations.

What was done couldn't be undone.

"Look, if you aren't planning on writing me a citation and we're done here, I need to go," Marie said, reaching her hand out for her license and registration that Emily was still holding. "May I put my gun back in my holster?" she asked, motioning toward the Sig sitting on the hood of the truck.

Emily's eyebrows shot up. Clearly, she wasn't used to someone she had just pulled over dressing her down. He couldn't help but crack a smile, but he tried to mask it in the shadows of the night.

There definitely was something about Marie that could have gotten him all wrapped up if he wasn't careful. There was a swagger to her that he'd seen in very few women, and even less that were even half as pretty.

"Why are you carrying a gun, Marie?" he asked, unable to remain silent any longer, regardless of the instructions Emily had given in regard to his being on the ride along.

Emily glowered at him.

"I don't think that is any of your damned business." Marie looked at him like he was gum stuck on the bottom of her shoe.

The look made him feel like the gum, as well.

"Actually, I would like to know," Emily countered, surprising him.

Marie paused as though she was trying to decide whether or not to snipe back or be gentle with the deputy. Her face softened, but only slightly. "First, I'm not trying to be rude, but this *is* Montana, everyone carries a gun here, so I think it's ridiculous you think it's okay for you to ask me that question when I'm just like everybody else. Which brings me to my second thought, that you're only daring to ask me because I'm a woman. Yet, that confuses me—you being a woman in law enforcement. I'm sure you face your own sexism and wouldn't wish to perpetuate any sort of harassment that could perceived to be along those lines."

Emily opened and closed her mouth as she struggled to rebound from the verbal slap.

"What is odd about it is that you aren't from Montana, according to your license, Mrs. Costa." He took the license from Emily's hand and stared down at the Virginia license like it was a written order. "You are a long way from home, in fact. I don't believe Virginia is quite as generous with their open carry laws as we are here in the west."

She reached over and pulled the license from his hand and stuffed it in her back pocket. "And you aren't a cop. We all have our riddles."

Emily dipped her chin in appreciation. "You do know you were going ten under the speed limit. I could write you a ticket, Mrs. Costa."

Marie took a step back from her as her jaw dropped. "You have to be kidding me. You admitted that you saw I was pulled over on the side of the highway. Of course I would be going slower than the speed limit for a minute. You wouldn't dare write me a ticket." Her lip quivered with anger. "And stop calling me missus."

"I'd call you something else, but I'd probably lose my job," Emily said with a smile.

There may have been something ten degrees wrong with him, but he was getting a kick out of everything that was happening—especially the bit about Marie not being a missus.

"Ladies, let's not," he said in hopes of deescalating what was an admittedly entertaining, but ultimately unhelpful strife. "Marie, seriously though, why were you pulled over in front of the ranch. We ask because earlier today we had some issues with safety involving a woman in a truck that was identical to the one you are now driving. That and your stopping made you a prime suspect."

"What happened?"

"A woman crashed the truck in through the front doors of a restaurant in hopes of hitting my brother and me. At least, that's what I believe. Before we could get to her, she backed up and fled the scene. The police in Missoula County have been trying to find her but haven't had any luck. We believe she may have followed us up here to the Flathead."

"Why would anyone want to hurt you?" Marie asked with an empathetic tilt of her head. The movement was almost too much or perhaps it was a touch out of character for the abrasive woman, and a red flag popped up, but he pushed down the niggle of warning.

She wasn't abrasive—she was just standing up for herself, and he liked that about her. He appreciated a woman who wouldn't take guff from anyone—not even a cop who was, in all honesty, overstepping.

"The better question is why you were stopped on the side of the highway," Emily interjected.

"I was just looking at what was happening out by that barn. I thought the circus was in town. Wanted to ride an elephant." There was a distinct snarl in her voice.

Emily reached down and unsnapped the Molle case holding her cuffs. He put his hand up, motioning for her not to get ahead of herself. "Can you work that pistol as well as you can run your mouth?" he asked Marie with a smirk, in hopes it would endear him to her.

She gave him an appraising glance. "If you're looking for someone to work security at your circus, you don't have to look any further—I mean, if that's what you're asking."

His smirk widened into a full smile, but Emily let out an annoyed huff. "Yes, we are always looking for another clown."

She threw her head back as she gave a hearty belly laugh. "You know, I think we may just get along fine. Just don't actually make me ride an elephant—I'm an animal lover at heart."

He chuckled. "You got it. I'll keep that in mind." His thinking turned dirty, and he thought of the one thing he wouldn't mind her riding. He had to look away in an effort to stop the heat from rising on his cheeks and giving his torrid fantasies away.

With confidence like hers, she was probably damned good in bed.

"If you guys are done flirting, we have work to do," Emily piped up, annoyed.

He wanted to argue and say that they weren't flirting, but he didn't bother. It didn't matter what Emily thought; she was wrong. He didn't flirt.

At least, he didn't think he was flirting.

He slid a sideways glance over at Marie in hopes of getting her take on Emily's accusation. Unfortunately she was looking toward the barn and all he could see was the red-and-blue lights splashing over her skin and reflecting off her eyes like they were at a drug-fueled techno club in Ibiza.

He could imagine her now, sweat covered and scantily clad in some stringy top and tight leather pants, her eyes closed as she worked her body in sync with the beat.

The heat returned.

That was it—he needed to get out of here. Or maybe he just needed to get some time alone. More, he had to get away from Marie. It had been a momentary lapse in judgment to invite her to come work at the ranch, but maybe he still had a chance to change her mind and save himself the misery of prolonged torturous longing.

Emily walked back to her car. "You coming or what, lover boy?"

At least she hadn't called him Bozo.

"If you want, you can ride with me. You can show me where to park and tell me more about this security gig," Marie said, her voice soft and supplicating. It pulled at him like invisible hands.

He rolled his neck, trying to instinctively free himself of this woman's grasp. It wasn't working. Looking toward Emily, he said, "We'll follow you in. If I'm not back in an hour, send in the troops."

Marie cuffed him playfully and then pointed toward the passenger side of her pickup. "You can't possibly think I'm dangerous. You are the one who offered me a job, *lover boy.*" She smiled, the action making her so strikingly beautiful in the cascading lights that his heart skipped a beat.

Emily clicked off her lights, saving him some of his agony as he climbed into Marie's truck. A car passed by them on the highway, and then Emily pulled up next to them in the squad car and gave them a turn of the hand, signing to head out. Marie nodded.

"So," he started, awkwardly, "is this your pickup, or is it a rental?"

"It's mine. Why?" She frowned.

"Overseas, in the sandbox, a pickup kinda like this is super common. Especially white. It's what all the bad guys drive."

"Is that another reason you profiled me as a bad guy?" she asked playfully.

"Are you one?"

"A bad *guy*? No. *Woman?* Maybe. You know what they say—semantics can be nine-tenths of the battle."

He didn't know who *they* were, but if he wasn't careful *this* woman would be his demise.

Chapter Four

The West Glacier Ranch was just like she had expected thanks to the research she had done online. It was homey and everything Montana was touted to be: Western with a side of conservative hippie. It was a strange amalgamation of cultures all wrapped up into one mountainous region that few ventured, except when they wanted to take photos of them playing in the snow in Glacier National Park or standing by the pools in Yellowstone.

The place seemed to have a series of unspoken rules, just like every other place she had ventured into around the world—things that couldn't be said and ways women couldn't act. She had definitely stepped into it when it came to the deputy, but thankfully her mark, Wade Trapper, had seemed to appreciate her charms. Hopefully she could make her way into the rest of his inner circle as well.

At least she had guessed right about him.

With a contractor like Wade, he was going to like one of two types of women—an unfiltered woman like she naturally was, or a sheepish people pleaser who would go out of her way to make sure he felt like the head of the household. It all depended on his level of narcissism. So far, he had seemed to have passed that test.

If anything, when she was forced to give report to Corey, she would have said Wade was surprisingly likeable.

He was good, very good. It was no wonder he was a contractor. If she had to guess, he worked as a negotiator or an interrogator. A man who could charm the pants off anyone was equally beneficial in either role. Heck, he could have been both if he was working for a small company.

From what she had been told and able to pull about the Vaquero Group, they ran about a hundred contractors strong at any one time. They'd recently taken a pretty hard hit in an incident in which he had been at the forefront. He'd taken leave, and that was how she had found her way here.

It wasn't unusual for a group to run investigations into their own contractors, not if they wanted to keep them. However, more often than not, if they sniffed that anything was even the slightest bit off with one of their players, that person would either be fired and shipped back to the States, or they would quietly disappear.

One call, and he still could be in the wind.

The thought made her squirm.

"This ranch has been in my family for generations," he said, not seeming to notice the emotional turmoil she was feeling. "My grandparents owned it, then my father took over, and now my brother, Cameron, and his wife are in charge—you met Emily." He motioned toward the squad car in front of them.

"She owns the ranch?" She was surprised. The hard-nosed cop didn't seem like a cowgirl.

"Don't let people's outward appearances confuse you—sometimes people aren't always what you make of them."

She gave him a quick once-over. "Would you say that's true about you?"

"Well, that all depends on the kind of guy you assume I am." He lifted a brow, giving her a flirty glance.

She didn't want to show him all of her cards—or even half of them, if she was being honest. "I think you are the kind of guy who knows how to make a woman like me blush." She smiled.

He laughed, the sound strong and filled with honest joy. "You come off tough, but then all I have to do is flirt a little and you go to blushing. You are a woman who's full of contradictions."

He had no idea.

"I like to keep a guy on his toes." She pulled her hair loose of its tight braid and let it fall free around her shoulders.

He stared at the long locks as they fell down over her breasts. "What kind of security did you work in? Are you a cop? Active? Or are you looking for another full-time thing?" He seemed to struggle in his attempt to look away but finally his gaze moved to her face instead of her hair.

"I used to be a city cop in Arlington."

He sniffed. "That had to be one hell of a job—being a city cop in a place built around the federal system."

"Federales weren't overly fond of us, but we generally left each other alone."

"I've heard some stories about their training simulations around the area. I can't imagine they didn't overstep into your territory." He sent her a knowing look.

"Oh, you heard about some of those, did you?" She smirked. "In all honesty, they do most of their active training in Hogan's Alley. It's a replica of a town where they role-play and are put in life-and-death situations they would face on the streets. It's the washouts that create the most problems for us. They hit the bars, angry and disenfranchised by their time inside the walls of Quantico."

His facial features tightened, and it made her wonder if she had struck a nerve. If she had, there could have been something to the theory of his having a role in the deaths of his friends.

"So you *used* to? What happened, if I may ask?" he pressed.

She would have hated the question if she had been telling the truth. In all reality, she had never worked in Arlington as a city cop—that had been her sister, Auriella, who was still there and loving every second of the gig. "I needed a change. The politics got to me after a while. I decided to take some time off and travel the country for a few months—it's how I ended up here."

He nodded. "I know how it feels to want to run away."

His admission surprised her. He didn't

seem like the kind of guy who opened up and poured out his feelings.

The crew was actively filming as they approached the barn and front pasture where she had first noticed the lights from the highway. As they grew nearer, there were barricades with yellow-and-white paint set up to keep people from walking into the filming areas.

She'd never been around anything like it before. Emily was standing beside a barricade with a man who was dressed in all black with *Security* in yellow emblazoned on his chest. He gave them both a nod as Emily waved them over.

Wade stumbled, and she reached for him, feebly attempting to keep him from flailing. "Are you okay?" she asked.

He straightened up, composing himself and dusting off his shirt, but he couldn't keep his eyes off Emily and the man. "Yeah. Fine."

She frowned. "What's wrong?"

He looked as though he had seen a ghost. "Nothing. I'm fine." He motioned toward the duo. "Let's go see what they need from us." He strode away, leaving her in his wake as though he had suddenly forgotten that she was even with him.

Following behind him like a lost duckling

she watched as Emily introduced the two men, calling the man in black James. The handshake between them was a second too long, and James's knuckles turned white as he gripped Wade. He slapped his other hand over their entwined hands. The body language came off as odd—it was usually an action which indicated sincerity, but in this moment, she couldn't help but wonder if it was instead to show dominance and authority.

Emily motioned for her to come closer. "James, this is our newest security hire. Meet your new addition, Marie..."

"Costa," she finished, realizing how little these people knew and how much they were willing to trust a single woman alone on the highway. It had been her luck and arguably could lead to their downfall—if she proved the allegations about Wade's actions were based on truth.

James barely looked away from Wade as he let go of the man's hand and gave her a shallow nod. "Marie."

The director called for a scene change, and there was a flurry of motion and actors as the crew broke loose between takes. A stunningly beautiful blonde came sauntering over toward them, smiling widely at Emily and giving her a wave. She was wearing a set of pointed ears and makeup that was vaguely reminiscent of Angelina Jolie's character in *Maleficent*.

If she had been trying to actually seduce Wade, she would have been concerned by her own appearance in comparison to the knockout who was costumed and staged to perfection in front of them, a woman whose role it was to enthrall millions through her art. This woman was damned good at her job, and she hadn't even really had the chance to see her act.

James looked at the woman as though she hung the moon, and he dipped his head in greeting as she approached. "Hello, Ms. Leafletter," he said with a smile. He pointed toward her. "This is Marie."

"Call me Scarlett. And charmed," Scarlett said, nodding in her direction. "The director wants to talk to you. Apparently, there is someone asking for you?" She motioned vaguely toward the director.

"Who?"

She shrugged. "He didn't say."

He turned to Wade, and his smile faded and his tone darkened. "As soon as I get off, we need to sit down and talk. I'll be done at midnight when they are finished shooting."

"Actually, I think we're wrapping up a bit early. I wouldn't be surprised if it is closer to eleven," Scarlett said. "There's a cute little bar not far from here—the Mint. A few members of the cast are going to meet up there later, if you want to meet us all there."

James nodded. "The Mint. Eleven. Until then, I've work to do." He gave a two-fingered wave as he retreated into the crowd of actors and actresses who were milling around, waiting for their next call.

She'd always hated the idiom that someone had looked like they had bit into a lemon, but there was no better way to explain it look on Wade's face. His lips were puckered and his face scrunched, and he looked exactly like he had a mouthful of its sour flavor.

"Don't worry about him," Scarlett said, waving the man off as he disappeared behind the barn. "He's always off somewhere. I swear he is constantly chasing after ghosts."

Something about the way the woman spoke made chills run down Marie's spine. "How long has he been working for your security team?"

"I don't know." Scarlett sounded nonchalant. "We've been filming here for about a month. I think he's probably been here for that long. I've seen him come and go at least for the last couple of weeks. I couldn't tell you for sure though. After a while everyone on the crew kind of blurs together. All I know is that I need to learn my lines, make money, and do right for the ranch." She let out a giggle.

She couldn't blame the woman for not keeping track of faces. In a job like Scarlett's, she had to see so many extras and crew members who came and went every day that to try to keep track of each would have been a Sisyphean task. Looking around, tonight there must have been at least two hundred different people working on the set between cast, crew, security, catering, and ranching staff.

"So," Emily turned back to Marie, "you were saying you worked in the private security world?"

Scarlett perked up. "That's interesting, I've been talking to my fiancé about hiring a private security officer. I wanted a woman." She looked to Emily. "Let me know how this goes with..."

She looked at her expectantly.

"Marie," she said, giving her name again.

"Yes, *Marie*. If you approve, Emily, perhaps that would be something I would be interested in pursuing. We can chat later though.

I need to run." The woman smiled at Emily but barely registered Marie and Wade as she whirled on her heel and hurried away.

If the starlet was always a flurry of motion, Marie wasn't sure that she would have wanted the job—that was, if she had actually been looking for a move from the Falcon Group. She liked the routine and the rigidity of her role in her current job. They let her do her thing, but they were on time and regimented, and she needed that level of structure or her anxiety had a way of creeping in and creating chaos in her mind.

Scarlett the starlet shook hands and smiled her way through the crowd of fellow actors and actresses. There was a man with the name *Anciaux* embroidered on his royal-purple jacket in gold lettering talking to her, and he looked in their direction. His pudgy face was dour and sweat beaded on his temples. He looked stressed and put out by the hold up in filming, and something about him made Marie wonder if he was the money behind the project.

Wade touched the back of her arm, making her jump and pull away. She made a strangled sound at his unwelcome and unexpected touch.

"Sorry," she said, trying to cover her misstep. "I forgot where I was for a moment."

"No worries," Wade said. "I bet you are tired. You said you've been traveling. Right?"

She nodded.

"Do you have a place you're staying?" he asked.

Emily rolled her eyes. "I'm going to go find your brother. Keep it above the sheets, you two."

Wade laughed. "Don't rain on our fun just because my brother must be holding out in the bedroom," he teased.

Warmth moved up Marie's cheeks. She had wanted to be included in the inner circle, but she wasn't sure she was ready for this level of inclusion quite yet.

"Oh," Wade said, seeming to notice her blushing. "I didn't mean to embarrass you. We are ranch kids through and through. Sometimes I forget others have better manners and weren't born in a barn."

She waved him off. "You're okay. I just… You're right, I'm just tired." She gave a weak smile. "And no, I don't have a place to stay yet. I was just going to keep driving until I was tired and then stop for the night."

"Where were you headed?"

"I was following the wind, trying to find myself," she lied. It felt so out of her real character that it nearly made her cringe. She wasn't the kind to go anywhere without a destination and a schedule that was so well-planned that there was little wiggle room for deviation.

"If I tried to find myself, this would be the first place I would look, too," he said, motioning toward the Montana mountains.

She hadn't thought about it, not really, but the man had a point. In the moonlight, the ephemeral silver gleam made them look like a white vertebral column—and it struck her that in many ways that is exactly what they were—the backbone of their world.

Chapter Five

When Wade had shown up on the ranch, the last thing he had expected was to walk right into a life and a world that seemed to be waiting for him. It was strange, but he had been welcomed and brought in as though he had never been gone. Perhaps it was all the action at the ranch that had created him a position, but he wasn't about to look at this gift horse in the mouth.

Emily felt like a sister, and she was everything that Cameron had told him she was—plus. If anything, he had downplayed just exactly how lucky he was. He still wasn't exactly sure how a schlub like his brother had managed to pull a deputy like Emily, who not only had her act together but had the wherewithal to put up with Cameron and the rest of his siblings.

Thinking about siblings… Scarlett, whose given name was Teri Trapper, was something else. He hadn't liked the way his sister had treated Marie, but then again, she had offered Marie a job—passively. Without the chance to talk to Emily or Scarlett, he wasn't sure exactly what to make of the statement—whether it was an empty nicety or a legitimate job. Regardless, he wished his sister would have talked to him quietly about it before she had gone ahead and put it out there.

Marie was a bit of a mystery. There was an air about the woman that he couldn't quite put his finger on that he didn't trust. He hated it, knowing it was probably his own lapse in character that made him feel that way, but he couldn't help himself. It was more than likely his job and his endless wars which had made this unending feeling of mistrust creep through him.

He hated that he couldn't be like everyone else and just blindly pass through life not knowing that danger was just a blink away. It didn't matter where a person lived or what they did for a living—in a second everything could change, the cars on the road could swerve, or the people they thought they could trust would turn against them in ways they had never even imagined.

At least he would never be taken by surprise, or so he hoped. Only a fool would let their hubris blind them to possible attack.

"Are you okay?" Marie asked, pulling him from his whirlpool of thoughts which had threatened to suck him down into the abyssal plains of his soul.

"Yeah, fine."

"And I'm Mother Teresa." She cocked a brow. "You going to tell me what is really eating at you?"

He chuckled, looking over at her in the floodlights that the film crew had set up around the paddock where they were shooting the next scene. Her hair looked almost purple in the glow, and it reminded him of his wilder days spent in the European clubs when he'd fallen in love with EDM, much to his teammates' chagrin. There was nothing quite rolling through the sandbox listening to techno at the highest volume and pretending the world around them didn't exist.

He'd kill for those days again.

Okay, maybe not exactly *kill.*

"What are you looking at?" she asked, shyly pushing a loose strand of hair behind her ear as she glanced away from him.

"I was looking at you and thinking that it's a good thing for me that you're not a nun."

She threw her head back in a laugh. "Who's to say I'm not."

"Angelic looking, maybe. But let's call a spade a spade—you're as dangerous as I am."

She shot him a look, and there was so much vitriol in her eyes that they told him he was right on the money. It also made him wonder if he was right in not trusting her.

As quickly as the expression had appeared it faded and she smiled, but the action was somehow violent. "I get the impression that the last kind of woman you would want in your life would be a doormat. You would walk all over the poor thing."

She wasn't wrong.

"Who says I want a woman?"

"If you want a man, I'm going to say the same thing. He'd better be an alpha."

He rolled his eyes, and he immediately hated himself for such a pubescent action, but he couldn't take it back. "I'm not interested in men. I love women, but I'm not looking for a relationship. That kind of thing isn't in the cards for me."

She nodded like she could understand, even perhaps felt the same, but she moved to the log fence in front of them and rested her arms on the top rail and started to tap her fingers together.

"You didn't like that answer?" he asked.

She looked over her shoulder at him as he approached. He didn't even bother to hide the fact that he had been caught staring at her perfectly round ass. Everything about this woman was attractive, even down to the way she snarled at him at each turn and didn't balk at his best attempts to keep her at arm's length.

He didn't know how, but her aversion to him only made him want her that much more.

Things with this woman weren't going exactly how he had hoped—that was, unless she was okay with keeping things *simple*.

He leaned on the fence rail beside her.

She sighed. "What is it about men?"

He ran his hand over the back of his neck. "What do you mean by that?"

She leaned back from him so she could look him directly in the eyes. "Just because I'm a woman and you're a man, that doesn't mean we just have to jump into some kind of *situationship* together. If you want me to be a part of this ranch and its security team, then we need to be careful. Like you said, if we call a *spade a spade*, then let's be honest and up-front—we are attracted to each other."

He let out an airy laugh that sounded like a surprised huff. "Oh." He squeezed the spot he had been rubbing.

The woman was direct; he would give her that.

"Sorry," she said, the blush in her cheeks returning. "I'm not *normal*."

"First, I don't know what you mean, and second, what's normal?"

She laughed. "My friends have politely let me know that I'm what they call 'quirky', but I call it being neurodivergent." She said the word with finger quotes. "I like to think of it as a way to say that I'm a unicorn—unique in all the best ways."

"Then I'm glad you're not normal."

Her smile widened. "Sometimes, so am I. Others…it's a challenge."

"We all have our challenges."

"Yes, but that is also a platitude. I hear it a lot." She covered her mouth. "Sorry. There I go again. I need to shut up or just say *thank you*. It would make life so much easier."

"We all have something in ourselves, platitude or not, that we don't like—or we wish to change. That's part of being human. It's only the real monsters out there who think they are perfect."

"I find that those are the monsters I seem to keep finding myself fighting," she said with a laugh. "That may explain why I'm so hard on myself sometimes. It would be simpler if I could just compartmentalize or become more like them. At least I could just focus on what needs to be done instead of being stuck in this ridiculous loop of self-reflection. I hate it sometimes."

He would have been lying if he had said he wasn't slightly taken aback by her candor. This wasn't a conversation he was sure he'd ever had aloud with anyone other than himself.

"I understand, more than you know," he answered simply, even though what he really wanted to tell her was that he had spent countless hours stuck in that same cycle, questioning choices he had made, things he had said, and then wondering how he should have done things differently—especially when it had come to that day when his teammates had been killed.

There was the faint smell of smoke in the air, but he wasn't sure if it was an illusion or if it was just the nightmares in his mind which made it seem real.

His thoughts turned to James, and he scanned the crowd, looking for his former teammate.

He still couldn't believe his friend had found him. Though Wade recalled telling him that his family had a ranch in Montana, he didn't think he had given him nearly enough information for the guy to hunt him down. If anything, it made a deep sense of unease fill him. If James could find him, there would be no telling who else could show up at the ranch as well.

Maybe coming back here had been a stupid idea.

If he thought he was putting his family in any sort of danger, he would have to leave.

First, he needed to sit down with James and see what had brought him to this corner of the world and why. It had to have been serious. The last thing he had heard about the man was that he was still actively doing contract work. If he had to guess, he had been most recently working in Ukraine, like many of his remaining friends in their business.

James was nowhere to be seen.

The cast was getting into their positions to resume shooting, and from behind the barn, there was a murmur of voices. A group of people walked out, two of them were wearing aprons filled with makeup brushes and one was frantically patting at Scarlett's face with some kind of makeup sponge.

He never understood all the primping and prepping women did, but he could appreciate the end results. His sister looked stunning, and if he couldn't have been prouder of how far she had come in the years since he'd last seen her as a gangly legged teen to the gorgeous and confident movie star she had become.

James stepped out from behind the barn and watched them from the shadows, his arms crossed over his chest.

"Marie, I'll be right back," he said, touching her gently on her shoulder as he sent her a smile.

She looked surprised that he was willing to cut their conversation short, but she gave him a small nod. He would have liked to have kept talking to the woman. She was great, but he didn't need to take things further—no matter how beautiful or ethereal she was. A woman like her could only bring him one thing: trouble.

Before he could change his mind, he turned away and made his way toward James. The man had disappeared back into the shadows behind the barn.

There was a swath of gravel around the barn to keep down the mud and mess from the steady flow of horses and riders, and the gate to the pasture was open. In the main pasture the crew had set up several new Jayco trailers, and it appeared as though they were for the makeup crew and wardrobe and maybe for the bigger stars to rest between takes.

It was a nice area, and if he was to be honest, he was a little bit jealous. It was a far cry from the Conexes that they'd used in the war zones, which were nothing more than the steel shipping containers that had been retrofitted to work as mobile homes for contractors in the field. Calling the steel boxes homes was definitely a stretch, as they were just for storing bunks and trunks.

He had perfected the art of living a minimalist lifestyle.

"Hey, man, you out here?" he called, hoping James would hear him.

He was answered with the murmur of the crowd in the distance and the chirping of the crickets in the night.

"James?"

"You know, it's a wonder we ever made it

out of Hawija and away from ISIS with you being this effing loud," James said with a laugh, stepping out from behind the farthest camper on the left.

He smiled and gave James a two-fingered wave as he made his way over to him. "I don't think it mattered how loud or quiet we were. We were just damned lucky."

"That's no kidding," James said with an affirming nod as he glanced around like he was looking to make sure they were alone. "That's actually why I was hoping to talk to you later."

"Oh?"

"I don't think it was just random that we made it out," James said.

He couldn't have heard James right. If what he was saying was correct, it could have had any number of possible implications. "What do you mean?"

"I think we're in trouble," James said, moving closer to him, as though he was going to tell him some torrid secret.

There was the strange but familiar sound of a high velocity projectile hitting its wet target.

No.

His imagination had to be playing tricks on him, and his nightmares were creeping into his reality. He looked down at his body, sure that he couldn't have been correct.

There were little speckles of red blood all over him. High-velocity blood spatter.

He looked at James.

His friend fell slowly to his knees, collapsing onto the ground in front of him. His head hit the ground just inches from his feet.

Wade drew his gun from his holster, readying himself for the gun fight he was sure was coming. Yet he had no idea where the shot had come from or who was shooting at them—or why.

There was the high-pitched scream of a woman. She sounded terrified, as if she was being attacked.

The sound made the hairs on the back of his neck stand, and he forgot himself and moved toward the sound like it was his personal call to arms.

Marie was looking at him in absolute horror.

"Wade...what did you do?" She looked at the pistol in his hands. She pulled her weapon from her holster and pointed it at him, making his heart nearly stop. "Drop your gun!"

Chapter Six

A droplet of blood dripped down the side of Wade's face, slipping down his temple as he stared at her. His finger was off the trigger, but one split second and a tiny movement and she would be dead. She hated that they were here, that they were at this impasse, and they were at this point.

"Drop. Your. Gun. Wade," she repeated, trying to keep her voice from wavering. He didn't need to have any clue that she was afraid.

Maybe he was afraid, too. Any normal human would be scared at this moment. In a single nanosecond a life could be forever changed, taken, or surrendered. It all came down to the feeling in her gut and the life and decision that she faced.

He lowered his gun, putting up his left hand in surrender. "It's not what it looks like. I swear." He moved to place his gun back into his holster, pointing at it with his left hand questioningly. "Okay?"

She nodded. "Slowly."

He moved like his life was on the line. He was right—it was.

The holster clicked as the pistol moved into place. He moved his hands up. The palm of his right hand had a smear of blood at its center, just where the grip of his gun had been a second before. She stared at the smudge.

"What happened here, Wade?" she asked, motioning toward James, who was face down in the grass just beside the gray-and-blue Jayco camper. Blood was creeping out from underneath his head and seeping into the ground around, darkening the soil beneath as the pool moved outward.

She stepped over to the fallen man and pressed her fingers into his neck. His flesh was warm, but there was no sign of life regardless of how hard she pushed.

The hole in the back of his head was larger than she would have expected for a handgun, but she glanced back at the weapon holstered on Wade's hip. "What're you shooting?" she asked.

"Glock 19."

"So, a 9mm?"

He nodded.

He could have been standing farther back when he'd shot James—it would have made for a larger-circumference entrance wound. Or it could have been a different gun entirely, and he had been telling the truth about firing the shot.

She hadn't heard the sound of a gun. He wasn't shooting suppressed. At least not the gun that she had seen in his hand when she had found him. It would have packed one hell of a punch and gotten everyone's attention if he had shot off a round. It couldn't have been him. Plus, the blood on his palm—it had to have been either on the grip of his gun or he'd had his hands up when James had been shot. Or he was really damned good at covering his tracks.

Right now, she had to believe he was innocent—and more, there was someone else out there firing off rounds from a suppressed weapon. And for all she knew, they were the shooter's next targets.

She took a quick series of photos of the body and the surrounding area. She wasn't quite sure why but knew that if she didn't, she might regret it later. This could very well be the last chance she had to see this man, and maybe there was something in the darkness she had missed—some clue that would lead them to answers later.

They weren't far from a set of brand-new Jayco campers, which looked as though they were likely set up and being used by either the main stars of the show or the makeup crew. The lights were off in them, and not even their exterior lights were on.

"Wade, let's go." She took motioned for him to follow her away from James and from the scene of the shooting. The last thing they needed was to stay in range.

As though he was thinking along the same lines, he put his arms over her shoulders and hunched down and hurried them away from the area and around the side of the barn. He slipped inside the barn doors and out of sight.

He moved her toward the back of the barn, where there was a stack of hay, and he pulled a bale from the top of the stack and put it down on the ground and motioned for her to sit. She did as he requested and as she sat, the bits of dried alfalfa stuck into her leggings and poked into the backs of her thighs like needles. It was still less uncomfortable than possibly being down range from a killer.

There was blood spatter on his jeans, or at

least a red blood-like substance she guessed was blood. It was so fine it was what she would have best described as having been misted across the cotton fabric. Where his hand had brushed the cloth, the crimson liquid had smeared and soaked in, looking like some macabre art piece.

His shirt was similar, but the higher she looked, the larger the drops became. The largest were around the area of his left shoulder. From the trajectory, that had to have been approximately the angle at which the projectile had moved through James's body.

"Where were you standing when James was shot?" she asked, still trying to make sense of exactly what had happened.

"I was standing pretty close to where you found me. Maybe a step or two closer… I don't know. Everything happened so fast."

That she could understand. In a firefight, things had a way of slowing down and a person often went into a dissociative state to compensate for the chaos happening around them. It helped them to myopically focus on what they believed could keep them alive.

It was strange, but when women had traumatic events, they could often tell a doctor or detective exactly what they were wearing, down to the color of their socks when they were attacked.

She knew all too well. The last time she'd been attacked, while she'd been in Oman, she'd ended up having to throw away her favorite Mac Duggal dress afterward. She couldn't look at its beaded corset top hanging in her closet without starting to tremble and sweat.

Even now, thinking about it, her hand started to shake.

"We need to find Emily and tell her what happened, get in a team to investigate." She hated it even as she suggested the idea, but it had to be done.

"Emily is going to be upset. She didn't want anything to happen—or as she put it, there was to be 'no unwanted attention.'"

"This will definitely be drawing scrutiny." There was no way around it.

A woman's scream filled the air—sounding from behind the barn.

Their gazes met. "Do you swear that you had nothing to do with what happened to James?"

He put his hand up like he was some kind of Boy Scout. "I swear on my life. The last thing he said was that we were in trouble."

"If I tell anyone what I saw, you are going to be spending the night in jail. Especially looking the way you do. You know that, right?" she said, motioning toward the blood on his clothing.

"But you have to know, you have to believe me when I say that I'm innocent," he begged. "And we are just wasting time in our search for the person who pulled the trigger if they drag me in. You know as well as I do that whoever is behind James's death is probably still out there. And they are either already on the road or waiting to get someone else in their sights."

"Do you know who would want to kill James? Or why?" she asked, thinking about why she had been sent there in the first place.

He shook his head, but there was a darkness in his eyes that had nothing to do with standing in the animal and hay-scented barn. There was something there, in his eyes, which told her she would need to dig deeper.

"We need to get you out of these bloody clothes and away from here, without letting anyone seeing you." She looked out at the people rushing by the front of the barn toward the sound of the woman's wail.

There was a tack room to her right. There,

just inside the door was a dark blue horse blanket. It was dirty and probably smelled, but it would have to do. She rushed over and grabbed it off the hook and carried it back to him. "Here—wrap this around you." She pushed it into his hands, and he did as he was told. "Now, where are you staying?"

She wasn't sure exactly how she felt about covering up the fact he had been so close to James's murder. If she was wrong and he did have something to do with the man's death, she was making herself an accessory after the fact. However, if she was right in believing him to be innocent, she was saving herself a great deal of time and was possibly saving any number of lives—and maybe even her own.

It was hard to know.

However, she had to trust her instincts on this one. The evidence that she had been presented with was strongly in Wade's favor.

As for his role in the deaths of the other men in Iraq, that was still to be decided, and she would get to the bottom of it, but for now and for his role in James's death she had to do what she felt was right—even if it was skirting what was legal.

"My brother got me set up in a trailer, just

like the ones out back. It's just down the road and along the river." He motioned vaguely toward the east.

"We need to make sure we aren't recognized or seen by whoever is out there and possibly gunning for us."

He nodded, slowly. "I hate to admit it, but if that shooter wanted to kill me, and if they were good, they had their chance. They could have taken me out back there."

"If they had the right line of sight. Who knows where they were set up? If they couldn't see you, they couldn't get a shot. There are a lot of variables at play, variables we don't know yet."

He pulled out his phone. "I have to tell Emily. I'll tell her that I'm going back to the trailer to change. If she wants my clothes and a statement she can find me there. At least that way, she won't think I'm hiding something."

Marie gave him the tip of the head in agreement. His sister-in-law wasn't going to like the move, but Marie had to give the guy props for giving her a heads-up. If he had done anything to hurt James, he would have been more than happy to keep things hidden. Once again, she had to think this man was innocent in James's death.

He tapped away on his phone as he walked toward the entrance of the barn. He slipped his phone into his pocket and then held out her hand to take it. “Let’s go.” He glanced around, watching to make sure no one was paying attention before they slipped out into the mask of darkness.

Chapter Seven

There had been so many battles in Wade's past that he couldn't begin to count them on two hands. However, he could count the number of times he had heard bullets ripping past him that closely. Normally, he had been wearing his ear protection and the sounds had come as pops. It was only a few times he had heard himself on the receiving end of suppressed fire.

Wade had fought countless battles in his past.

Insurgents rarely cared to hide their gunfire. They wanted the villagers and locals to know they were fighting and killing. They wanted to instill fear in the foreigners.

It was generally men like him, contractors and Americans who liked to use suppressed weapons. It kept their positions secret and their enemy unaware that they were even in the area and bearing down on their targets.

Which made Wade have hope that whoever was behind James's death wasn't coming for him.

James's last words haunted him as he changed his bloody clothes inside his bedroom in the camper while Marie waited in the main area. He folded his pants and shirt and left them on the sink as he took a quick shower and dried.

It felt good to be clean, but no matter how hard he dried his body, he could still feel the specks of blood on his skin. No doubt, it would take some time for the sensation to recede.

He looked at his hand where the blood had pooled in his palm. He would need to wipe down his gun.

The thought made his knot of emotions hitch in his throat. He couldn't explain why. This wasn't his first experience with death of a friend. It wasn't the first time he'd had to wash a friends' blood from his body. Perhaps, it was that it was here, at his *home* in Montana. Their enemies had followed them here, to the one place he thought he could be safe.

James had been working for the film crew before he arrived, but that wasn't to say the shooter hadn't followed Wade to the ranch.

Either one of them could have brought the wolf to the sheep.

He would carry the weight of not knowing who caused this forever. And if someone else got hurt, or killed because he had come home…

"Wade? Are you okay?" Marie called, almost as if she had some sixth sense for his self-flagellation.

"Just fine," he lied.

"Fine. Uh-huh." She called out the lie, and he had to admit he liked her more for it, though he'd never tell her that aloud.

There was a loud banging on the camper door that made the whole thing shake. "Answer the damn door. Now!" Emily's voice echoed through the thin aluminum walls.

The bathroom door's hinges squeaked as he stepped out and readjusted his shirt. "Hold your horses. I'm coming," he called, sending Marie an apologetic look.

Marie simply shrugged and put up her hand in resignation, as though she wasn't even a tiny bit surprised that his sister-in-law was standing outside the trailer and about to rain terror.

As soon as he unlocked the door, Emily came storming in like she was hell on wheels.

"What were you thinking leaving the scene? Do you know what it looked like that you rolled out? You're putting my job on the line!" Her face was so red that she was nearing purple. "Your brother is going to have your ass as soon as I tell him what you have done."

"EM," WADE SAID, his voice smooth and sedate, "why don't you sit down and have some water. You know as well as I do, I had to do what I did. I saved all my clothes for you, if you want to verify my story. You can question me and Marie until we turn blue. You will see that we had nothing to do with James's death."

Nothing to do with his death may have been a little bit of a stretch, but they may not have pulled the literal trigger.

Emily stared at him like he was holding an assault rifle that was pointed right at her. "You need to tell me what the hell is going on. The truth. No holding back."

Now they were getting somewhere.

"What do you want to know?" He closed the bathroom door and sat down at the table. He appeared as if he was readying himself for interrogation.

"Your brother may not have cared why you came back, but I do. Why did you come to

Montana? Are you still actively working? Or, are you done?"

His face darkened and his gaze flickered to Marie then down to the table. "I don't have an answer for whether I'm working or not. Am I officially retired? No. Do I have another job lined up? No."

Emily shoved her thumbs under her Kevlar vest beneath her Sheriff's uniform. "So…are you here for some vacation? Or, are you running from something?"

"Em, we're all running from something." He laughed. "As for vacation, if you look around, working with my sister is a long way from being a holiday. That woman is a handful. I came back because I thought I could catch my breath and make some decisions about my future." There was the ring of truth in his voice, but Marie didn't completely buy his answer.

"You said you knew James."

"Yes, we worked on a team together in Iraq. He and I lost a lot of brothers when we were on a classified mission. That's all I can say. Anything more and you're both going to need some higher security clearances. In fact, be grateful I'm telling you that much."

He wasn't wrong. She wouldn't have told

anyone a thing about her work in the field, and she certainly wouldn't have admitted to having worked with another person—dead or alive. She wouldn't have compromised another person's identity.

However, she was glad that he was willing to open up, it was saving her so much investigative work—and, for good or bad, she found herself liking him.

"Can you tell us how the men died?" Marie asked.

He jerked slightly. "I can't. However, I can say it's not uncommon for people in my line of work to die. To be completely honest, I never thought I was going to set foot back on American soil. I'd even put together my will before I took the assignment."

She knew that feeling all too well.

"Do you have any enemies that you know of? Or, at least that you can tell me about?" Emily pressed.

He looked down at his hands. "I have so many enemies, I don't even know where to begin."

Emily sighed, she sounded tired. "Anciaux doesn't want to stop rolling to call in the coroner. I'm not giving him an option. Right now, I have another officer holding the scene while we wait for the rest of my team to arrive. I won't tell anyone about your being near James at the time of his death, but if it comes out that you knew him and that you worked with him, I'm not going to lie for you."

He nodded. "I appreciate it."

"And if they find out that you were there, expect trouble."

"I won't say a word about you, or that you knew a thing. In fact, you were never there at the time of his death. But I promise, Marie and I are going to work to find out who was behind this. We won't stop until we get our hands on the killer."

"Good. I expect that you will use all of your *clearances* to get to the bottom of this. If you don't, I'll personally make sure you don't stay on this ranch for another minute. If you're bringing problems to this family, I don't care how much everyone loves you—including myself—you can't be here." Emily's voice quaked, but her face was stoney.

"If I don't have answers for you in the next forty-eight hours, I will be out of here and on the next plane back to the sandbox." And his will would be sitting on his brother's desk, as he doubted that if he went back his luck would continue and he would once again survive.

She walked to the camper door and took one look back at them. "And you two—" she paused "—be careful." There was something in the way Emily spoke that made it clear what she really meant was *hands off each other.*

She slammed the door shut behind herself on her way out.

Emily hadn't needed to tell him to steer clear, he was more than aware. However, it did make him nearly chuckle. If she thought telling him not to do something was the way to get him to stop, she clearly didn't understand the style of Trapper men.

"Did you hear *that* too?" Marie asked, barely above a whisper.

He nodded.

"To be clear," she started, "there is no chance on this green earth that you and I will be a *thing.*"

He would have been lying if he hadn't felt a bit crestfallen at her proclamation. Yet, at the same time the sensation was followed by a sense of relief. If they weren't going to be a thing, then he didn't have to worry about the sexual tension that lay between them. Surely, it would still be there, she was a beautiful woman but at least the expectations—or lack of them—were out in the open.

"Perfect," he said, letting out a forced sigh. "I was so tired of you looking at me like I was a dancer from Thunder from Down Under."

She threw her head back with a laugh as she cuffed him gently on the shoulder. "You think you're tough stuff, don't you?" She opened the refrigerator door, grabbed a bottle of water, and then took a sip. "You know it's a wonder any woman could put up with you, with an ego like yours."

He didn't want to tell her how long it had been since he had been in a real relationship. If he did, he feared it would only help strengthen her argument. No woman out there *had* ever wanted to deal with him, and he couldn't blame them. He was a lone wolf, a man who traveled too much, who had too many emotional wounds, and battles in his heart. Why would anyone want him?

"Oh, Marie, I know."

Her face fell and he could tell she instantly regretted teasing him and he felt bad for saying a word.

"I'm sorry, Wade, I didn't mean it like that.

I went too far. Any woman would be lucky to have a man like you."

He sent her a crooked, half smile. "Oh, wow, that was a quick turnabout." He walked to her and took the bottle of water from her and took a drink before handing it back. "Tease away. I just had a moment. If you didn't tease me, I would actually worry that you didn't like me."

"Oh, you are that kind of friend?" she asked, with a smile.

"I'm the kind of friend who, once we are friends, you're never going to have to question. I'm loyal to the death."

There was a flicker of pain in her face and his thoughts returned to James. Maybe it had been too soon to say something like that in front of her, but it was true nonetheless.

"Speaking of friends, before all hell breaks loose, I want to get into James's place and see if we can find anything that can point us toward his killer," he said, grabbing his cowboy boots and slipping them on and pulling his jeans on over the tops.

"Do you know where he was staying?" she asked.

He pulled out his phone and texted Scarlett's fiancée, Miles, who had taken on the role as the main ranch hand, asking him about the location of James's residence. It only took a few moments before Miles hit him back with a GPS pin with the exact location.

Wade clicked on the pin and pulled it up on the map. It was within walking distance through a series of cattle trails, or they could get on the main road and take the ranch pickup. They also had her truck, which reminded him of the woman from the diner. Was it possible that the woman in the white Tacoma was their killer? How had the possibility that these two events being connected now only now struck him?

"Dude." He sucked in a breath.

"What?"

"The woman who tried to run me down. I bet it's the same one who shot James."

Marie's eyes widened with surprise. "We need to find her. If we can, maybe we can stop her before she has the chance to kill again."

If they didn't, there was one thing he could be sure of—he was going to be the killer's next target.

Chapter Eight

Wade walked toward the wall tent that served as James's living quarters. Apparently, his sister and Miles had stepped up in getting Wade a camper instead of the dirt-floor special. Most of the support staff and some of the extras who'd been granted special permissions were camping in canvas wall tents in a separate area near the river in a line alongside James. It looked similar to a wildfire fighter's camp with its blocky setup of white square tents. The only difference were the black chimneys poking out of the roofs and the lack of yellow-and-green clad firefighters milling around.

If anything, the place was quiet—almost too quiet.

Perhaps it was because the cast and crew were up at the main area of the ranch and shooting for the day. Plus, it was late enough that if people weren't taking part in today's shoot, then they were probably already tucked away in their glamping quarters.

Using the coordinates, he located James's tent. Unzipping the canvas, he opened the flap. It was warm and stale inside, and it carried the scent of trampled grass and overturned dirt.

"I can go in first, if you want," Marie said, motioning inside like the place contained a possible landmine.

She didn't know him if she thought he would send another person in to do his job—especially if that other person was a woman who he felt he needed to shield. Not that he would ever utter those words to her face—he had a feeling she would take his protectiveness just about as well as being put up on a shelf.

"You just wait there." He touched her arm gently and gave it a light squeeze. "I doubt it will take me long to look around. Besides, I don't think you want to have your fingerprints on anything. I bet Emily and her crew will get here to look for answers at some point. We don't need them looking in our direction."

Marie's face twitched. "Yeah. You're right."

He bit back a chuckle and the desire to make a joke about how long it had been since he'd heard anyone tell him he'd been right about anything.

There was a faux-zebra-skin rug on the ground, and it was pushed all the way to the entrance. To the side of the open flap were a pair of James's Ariat cowboy boots, one of them flopped over on its side, revealing its battered, dirty and worn sole. Beside them was a pair of camouflage Crocs that made him cringe. As comfortable as the shoes looked, he would never stoop so low as to buy a pair.

"You don't like them?" Marie asked, laughter flecking her voice.

"What?" He looked up from the plastic shoes that were just one fashion level above the beige grippy socks hospitals handed out.

"You're not a squishy-shoe fan?"

"You noticed?"

She giggled. "You can't judge them until you wear them. I'm telling you—they are the most comfortable shoes you will ever own."

"Oh, don't worry—I'll never own them, so I'll never know." He smirked.

There was a black duffel bag sitting on top of a wooden crate at the end of the white linen-covered bed. On the antique-looking crate near the head of the bed was a lantern and a switch that must have been connected to the black-and-brass chandelier that hung down from the center of the tent. There was a black iron fireplace set up in the corner of the tent for heat, and in the opposite corner was a table with a fruit basket and a wine fridge filled with whites.

There might have been something to this glamping thing after all. The camper was nice, but it was a far cry from a zebra rug, a hand-picked wine fridge, and chandelier. There was a briefcase on the floor beside the fridge, but it was the kind made of hard plastic and kept closed with a series of numbered locks.

It would be easy enough to walk away with James's computer and he could probably get in the case with the right tools and time, but he didn't have the tech background to worm his way into the computer effectively and then get out without being found. In fact, if he tried to get into that computer, he would probably have a team of killers knocking on his camper's door before he even got done closing out the active window on the screen.

He would just have to hit Emily up for information and hope that she would be willing to share. Though he hadn't been around her long, he hoped she knew that he stood on the family's side—and in this case, whatever side it was that kept their family safe.

The twin bed was perfectly made, without a single wrinkle in the pillowcase and exposed edge of the sheet folded neatly over the top of the down comforter. A violet lay on the pillow as though a member of the cleaning staff had made their way around the tents and straightened up like they were hotel rooms at a five-star resort.

A lot had changed on the ranch since he'd last stepped foot on the place.

He moved to the bed and picked up the flower, taking in its sweet floral scent.

When he'd decided to leave, his father and brother Ben were still alive and kicking—and running the place like it was a busted wagon wheel, complete with exploitation and money laundering.

He had thought going into contracting would lead him away from the chaos of Montana and a toxic family and he would find purpose and work for the greater good. As it had turned out, it had been just a larger and more corrupt game that had paralleled what had been happening at home.

If he had known the truth when he had tried

to escape Montana, he wasn't sure he would have made the same mistakes—especially not knowing what he did now, and especially not after having just watched one of his friends bleed out in front of him.

He had to find out who was behind the trigger and why.

If James had wanted to talk to him, and he had come so far looking for him when just a simple phone call or email would have worked, it must have been something serious—and he must have known his life was on the line. Which meant that he had to have left some kind of breadcrumb trail for Wade to gain information in the event of a catastrophic outcome—like that which had happened.

Wade just had to look hard enough to find what needed to be found and for what James had left for him.

He threw the violet back onto the bed and grabbed James's duffel bag. He dropped it next to the flower, and there was something strangely perverse about the juxtaposition between the harbinger of spring and fresh beginnings and the dead man's bag. He tried not to think about it, but his gaze kept flickering back to the dainty purple flower.

Unzipping the bag, he rifled through the

rolled and folded shirts and pants. James had kept his personal items to a minimum and only what he had needed to function. If a person was to set his bag next to James's when they were working, it would have been hard to tell them apart. But Wade always kept a picture of the mountains of Montana in the side pocket. It had started as a way to remind him of what and who he was fighting for but over time it had lost its luster and as the corners had started to curl and fray, and it had become merely a token of good luck.

In the distance, he could hear music playing. The song "Hell is a Dance Floor" by Vincent Mason filled the air and ran its fingers over the grass tops as it filtered down to the river and fell silent into the babbling water.

He looked over his shoulder at Marie, wondering if she was struck by how strange this moment of searching felt. There was an air of ethereal beauty in the lull of the tune and the scent of the dirt and lingering sweetness of the flower. Yet behind it all was the darkness of the night and the brutality of the life and loss which had brought them here.

How quickly things could disappear, lives could be erased, and fear could creep in through the cracks created by the losses.

In the bottom of the bag, he searched the edges looking for Velcro or a false bottom. Anything or anywhere that James could have tucked something private away. It was a long shot, but James would have known that he was a bit of a Luddite when it came to tech, and if he wanted Wade to find anything, it had better be something tactile.

Almost as if it was some kind of sign from the universe, there was the crinkling of paper from under the fabric beneath his touch. He dumped out the rest of the contents of the bag onto the bed and, using the chandelier's light, searched the seam of the bottom of the bag until he found a tiny hole about an inch wide. He stuck his finger inside and swept around until he felt the folded paper.

Careful to keep his back to Marie, he tugged the white sheet out from the duffel. It was a tiny piece of paper, no bigger than his palm, and as he unfolded it, he was met with a series of three pictures—two blondes and a brunette, all women.

Two of the women were strangers to him. Yet the woman at the far right…

He stopped himself from making a noise as he stared at the face in the center of the page—from the pointed nose to the long, blond hair and bright blue eyes, there was no confusing the woman for anyone besides the woman who stood directly behind him. But why would James have hidden a picture of Marie?

He flipped the paper over, hoping for some written explanation for the photos, but there was nothing. No warnings. No accolades. No names.

James had been concerned about these pictures enough to have hidden them in a secret compartment and in a way that Wade was sure James had put them there as insurance in the event of his death.

This had to be James's hit list, or something similar.

There were too many coincidences. Marie just randomly pulling over on the side of the road with the white Tacoma after he had been attacked that morning with a truck of the same make and model by a woman who looked similar… He stared at the pictures. He couldn't be sure, but was it possible that it had been one of the others? Maybe the other blonde?

"Everything okay?" Marie asked.

His entire body grew rigid, but he tried to force himself to relax in attempt to not give his thoughts away. "Yeah."

"What did you find?" she asked, stepping inside the tent and moving toward him.

"Nothing." He stuffed the paper into his pocket before she had the chance to catch a glimpse. "We need to get back. Emily is going to be here any minute with her team." He stuffed James's gear back into his bag and threw it back onto the crate, not giving a damn that things were in disarray.

All he could think about was how quickly things had just blown up in his life and how—just like that—the woman Wade had come to trust had just become his worst enemy.

Chapter Nine

“Stay right here,” Wade said, pointing toward the place by the fence that stood well out of sight from where James’s body lay.

Emily and her investigators were working on the scene, taking measurements and making notes.

They had set up floodlights on the area, blasting it with so much light that it made it almost appear like midday instead of the middle of the night. The evidence tech was taking photos, but there was a black tactical bag sitting beside her that was slung open and exposing a variety of tools and kits.

It was interesting to Marie to get to see this side of the attack. In her line of work as a contractor, she was normally in and out, and—if required—she would hear how things shook out after the fact to make sure her name was clear, but nothing further.

That wasn’t to say Marie hadn’t been

around her fair share of death. She most certainly had. The smell, the dank gray scent that came with the encroachment of unchecked bacterial growth and decay didn't bother her—not until it went into the advanced states of bloat and bugs. Then she wouldn't have been human, or a non-scavenging animal, to not have a natural aversion.

Given all she had experienced, it was almost comical Wade thought he needed to keep her at arm's length from the man in the pasture. If he didn't think she could handle it, he had another think coming.

Yet there was another part of her that she would never admit to a living soul that loved that a man would go out of his way to protect her and be the alpha. She was so used to being the one in control and being the one who was always taking the lead that it was a welcome reprieve from having to take one more hit on the soul.

She was tough and she could take all the hits she needed—she bounced—but it was nice not to have to worry about the recovery. In her years in contracting, she had come to think of death and trauma in the same context as the breakdown that came with exercising. When a person worked out hard, they incurred microfractures in their bones and tears in their muscles, each of which required the body to heal. With each injury, the body built thicker muscle and denser bone—and a better, stronger, and more resilient body.

There was no real difference when it came to the heart and soul. Repeated trauma created opportunities for growth, if only a person allowed themselves to recover and heal. And ultimately, just like working out, she had to want to have to go through the pain to achieve the reward. Sometimes it was easier to just become comfortable in her complacency.

On the other hand, ever since they had left James's tent, Wade had been *off.* She couldn't put her finger on exactly why or how, but there had been a significant change in the way he moved around her. It was as if the softness he'd had for her had disappeared, but she didn't know why.

She had asked him what had happened and if he had found something, but he'd sworn there had been nothing. And when she'd come in, all she had seen was the clothes on the bed and one smooshed delicate violet.

Yet there was a pain in her gut that told her there was more.

Had her cover been blown? Or was she just

looking for something that wasn't there and working herself into a paranoid frenzy?

Wade was talking with Emily, her hands were moving animatedly, and they appeared to be arguing—once again.

For not being siblings, they certainly fought like they were.

The coroner was standing near James's body and taking measurements. The evidence tech walked over to him and said something she couldn't hear, but they both looked in Wade's direction.

In all honesty, Marie was surprised Wade had wanted to come back to the scene of the shooting. If it had been up to her, they would have been looking around the area and trying to find where the potential shooter had been posted in hopes they could have narrowed down the trigger puller's identity.

The fact that it hadn't been his next move concerned her. He had to deal with an attack in a way similar to her, yet he was breaking from their training script—which meant she didn't know something he did. Which meant he must have found something in James's tent that he hadn't told her.

He was hiding something from her.

He didn't trust her.

Marie could wholeheartedly understand.

However, that didn't change the fact that she needed to know more.

There were the sounds of footfalls crunching in the gravel from behind her and a woman cleared her throat. "You doing okay?"

Marie turned, and there was a woman in her mid-fifties wearing a leopard-print top and black leather pants studying her. There was a bandage around her right hand's knuckles. The woman looked as out of place on the ranch as a flamingo in the Arctic.

"I'm okay. You?" She didn't quite know how to respond to the stranger.

"I'd like to say this is the first time I've dealt with a dead body on a shoot, but that wouldn't exactly be the truth. The other time, though, it was a drug overdose in the bathroom between takes. I found her." She shuddered at the memory.

"Oh, that's terrible," Marie said, trying to sound genuine, but it came out all wrong even to her.

The bottle brunette stuck out her hand. "I'm Kim, by the way. Kim Gonzalez. I'm Rick Anciaux's personal assistant. Wherever he goes, I go. It's the most codependent relationship I've ever had with a gay man and—"

she laughed "—the healthiest relationship I've ever had."

"Oh." She wasn't quite sure how to respond to this uncomfortable woman. It was as if she was talking to a walking cocklebur and all she wanted to do was get away.

"Did you know the guy?" Kim pointed at James.

"I'd just met him. You?"

Kim tipped her head and waved her hand nonchalantly, like she and James had been friends and yet she wasn't necessarily bothered by his passing. "He had been working for the crew for a couple of weeks now. He'd been going to the bars with Rick and me after we wrapped. Real quirky guy, if you ask me. Not that I know a thing. Besides, I'm not really one for gossip."

The number one rule of gossip was that any person who said they weren't one for gossip was the royalty of it.

The word *quirky* stung slightly, and she tried not to take it personally, even though she had been called that thousands of times over her lifetime. She sent a sideways glance toward Wade, hoping he hadn't decided she was *too* quirky for him and that was why he was acting so strange.

He didn't look at her. In fact, he hadn't looked at her since James's tent.

"What do you mean that James was different?" she asked, avoiding the trigger word.

"I found him snooping around in the trailers. He said he was just making sure everything was secure, but I told him he couldn't go in anyone's private quarters without asking in the future."

Her stomach tightened. "How did he respond?"

"He didn't seem to mind, which put my mind at ease—you know. He told me he had reason to believe there was a bomb somewhere in camp. I could hardly be upset that he was doing his job. Yet after that I never saw him going in another camper or tent again—and there were no more complaints from cast or crew."

There was something in the way the woman spoke, telling her about the bomb after the warning which struck her as odd. It was almost as if the woman had made the bomb an afterthought. If it had been her, the threat of a bomb in a public area—especially one in which her company would have been liable for any harm—would have been of utmost concern.

"Wait, you called James quirky, but now you're saying he was looking for a reported bomb." She paused, studying the woman and the way her blinking rate had suddenly rapidly increased.

"So?"

"Don't you think that would be normal behavior for someone you had hired as security? This searching for a bomb and going through trailers?"

The woman huffed.

Emily hadn't said anything about a bomb—not that she had been around very long, but certainly Wade would have told her about a threat of that caliber.

The woman was lying to her.

"Did he say who called in the bomb threat?" she asked, not calling out the lie and instead letting Kim run with it.

"He didn't say," she said with a shrug. "I'm just glad he didn't find anything. After that, we just left one another alone." She smiled, but it seemed as fake as the woman's hair color.

"So, you don't know who would have wanted James killed?" she asked, surprising herself with her bluntness.

The woman stepped back like the question had come with a fist. "No. No idea." She glanced around like she was searching for an exit. The director was walking toward them, chatting with one of the male actors, a tall and handsome blond with a white linen shirt and black pants that made him look like he was a former dancer for Chippendales—all he was missing was the clip-on bow tie and some rhythmic music.

She couldn't begrudge the director for his taste in men.

"James, yoo-hoo," Kim called, complete with a flourish of her fingers. "Over here."

He sent her a wave and exited his conversation with the sexy actor with a brilliant, toothy smile and a touch to the bicep. He strode over to them. "I see things are coming along in the investigation." He glanced down at his gold wristwatch. "I'm hoping they can get things wrapped up by morning. I have an investor meeting this week, and I need to make sure that we have enough raw film to show them to keep them happy."

Kim looked toward her. "Did you hear anything about how long you think this would take to clean up?"

She tried not to visibly cringe at their insensitivity. Here was a man who had just been shot, and they were only worried about when they could get back to work and how they could impress people.

"Well, James was shot, so…"

Anciaux sucked his teeth with a loud, annoyed click. "Look, I think this guy had a gun and wanted to end things. Considering his work, he was probably having a mental health crisis. You know these ex-military types… they're all PTSD-ed up and looking for a way to make a statement. I mean, who even hired him?" He rolled his eyes.

Marie's hands balled into tight fists, and she took a step toward the man but reminded herself that she was there to do a job for the US government. The last thing she could do was take a swing at a director for running his mouth and get her ass landed in jail for the night. She didn't need to draw any undue attention, no matter how badly the man deserved to swallow a couple of teeth.

Though she wanted to tell the man off and explain to him that just because someone chose their profession, it did not immediately mean that they were devoid of feelings or that they were riddled with guilt for the jobs they had completed. Military contractors weren't just killers. Among their many duties were recovering victims of kidnapping, trafficking operations, and slavery—in short, they were often the ones tasked with seeking justice for the people who couldn't. In this particular case, she was seeking answers for the families of men who had died under mysterious circumstances—similar to, but not the same as, James.

It was her hope she could find answers and bring solace to those who needed it while making sure nothing like the execution of the three men would ever happen again.

The United Nations couldn't be in the business of collateral damage, especially not when it was linked to the theft and failure to recover three hundred million dollars in gold bullion stolen from an Iraqi bank which had been destroyed by heavy bombing. The last series of missiles had penetrated the vaults. One could assume the bombing wasn't entirely an accident.

Leaked images of the incident had made it appear as those behind it were armed with American weapons and had gotten into an Escalade similar to that which had been blown up the day of the execution. Only a handful of people had walked away. The Iraqi government had threatened oil and gas sanctions on Europe and the US if the gold wasn't recovered or there was some form of restitution.

Political figureheads were watching from around the world and all wanted answers.

She couldn't bear looking at the naive director. Not only did he have no idea what he was talking about, but he was in over his head. James's death wasn't going to be something he could conveniently sweep under the rug.

Only a moviemaker would think real life could be so simple.

"I think you'll find James was not the one who pulled the trigger," she said, turning her back on the infuriating director and his minion.

She didn't have time to deal with people like them—she had more urgent business to attend to. In fact, if she didn't get answers soon, not only would her boss at the Falcon Group be breathing down her neck, but she wouldn't be surprised if she started to hear rumblings about Iraqi hitmen coming for anyone who had remotely been involved with the gold's disappearance and they would stop at nothing—and no amount of death would assuage their anger until there were answers and a resolution.

Marie strode to the fence and slipped through the rails, careful to stay out of the immediate possible crime scene, she stepped toward Wade. He was standing alone, watching the evidence tech as she started to work on what appeared to be the trajectory of the bullet. She had a long rod and a GPS device she was using to scan the immediate area. Marie moved beside him and put her hand on his shoulder in quiet support of what she knew he had to have been feeling. Death was always hard.

"Again, I'm sorry. Does Emily have any new information?" she asked.

He shook his head, but again, his gaze wouldn't meet hers and the knot in her gut returned.

The realization of what implications this man's death could have on their immediate future struck her hard. Any number of things could have happened here, none of which would have been good. Worst possibility of all, there was another gray man here—either from the American government, European, or the Iraqi side. If they were from the ally side, they had come with the intention of keeping James quiet. Either way, Wade was likely the next on the hit list.

If a killer had been sent here to make her work faster, they had done their job well. Yet their one possible mistake was not realizing that she'd grown to like Wade and wished to keep him out of harm's way.

"Did they find out anything about the shooter?" she asked.

He shook his head.

She looked over her shoulder to see who was watching them. The investigation team were all working away and Emily was talking to the coroner. The coroner was nodding, and there was the occasional word she could make out from their conversation and she could string together that they were planning on having the deputized coroner take the body to the medical examiner's office for further analysis. There was hope the bullet was still in the man's body so they could use it as evidence in tracking down their killer.

"Did they find anything in Wade's possession that could help us figure out what he wanted to talk to you about?" she whispered, making sure her voice was low enough that the Hollywood crew couldn't hear.

Wade cringed slightly. "No."

At least he was almost speaking to her, even if it was curt.

"What in the hell is going on, Wade? What happened? Why are you acting like this to me? Did I miss something? Did I upset you?" She hated the way she sounded so weak, but she couldn't keep up skirting around his anger toward her. She couldn't fight when she didn't know the rules of engagement.

He scowled at her, looking her up and down as though he was weighing and measuring her for their bout. "I'm trying to figure out who you are and why you really came to this ranch. It can't just be coincidental that everything started to go sideways the moment you arrived in West Glacier."

Her breath caught in her throat. This wasn't her fault. Not even close. If anything, this was *his.* She wouldn't even have been here if he hadn't been involved in the loss of the gold.

"Don't forget that I'm the one who found *you* with blood all over your hands. How *dare* you come at me with that kind of unfounded accusation? Do you even understand the implications of what you just said?"

His eyes narrowed. "You're not just some beat cop from Arlington. All you've done to me since you got here is lie. Now you want me to *understand* you. The only thing I want to do is to tell you to get the hell off this ranch and a world away from me." He spat the words with such anger that it forced her to retreat from him a few steps.

"You're right—I'm not just some *beat cop*

like you so colorfully put it, but you're wrong in thinking that I'm not on your side."

He took her by the arm and led her away from all the prying eyes and toward his ranch pickup. "Who in the hell are you, *really*? And why are you here? If you don't tell me, it's likely you will end up just like James."

"Are you threatening me?" she asked.

"I told you I didn't kill my friend. You know it as well as I do. Knock it off."

She did know, but she couldn't control the fight in her core. It was easy to throw that grenade in an attempt to avoid the bomb that was her truth.

She sighed resignedly. "The director thinks that James's GSW was self-inflicted—PTSD and attention seeking. He is a real peach."

"He said what now?" Wade snarled, he didn't even wait for her to explain, and he tore off toward Anciaux and Kim.

She followed Wade. It had been provocation on her part, to tell him what had been said, but it took some of the heat off her and that was exactly what she needed right now. He'd come far too close in asking too many questions about her job and her real reason for finding her way onto the ranch.

It wouldn't be long before he would want more answers.

He was already laying into the director. "Look, I don't care who you think you are, but it's my friend's body lying out there in the grass. If you think you can stand over here and talk nonsense about him while his body is still warm, then I will personally make sure the next set of remains the coroner will be handling are yours."

The director's face blanched, but he puffed up after a second like he was some kind of stunted pufferfish. "I don't know *who you think* you *are*," he countered, seething, "but you cannot and will not talk to me that way. I'm in control, and this is my set. I make the decisions around here."

Kim made a slight chicken-like clucking noise.

Wade stepped closer and looked down at the purple-jacketed man. "My family owns this ranch. If you want to continue your work here—"

Marie put her hand on his arm, stopping him mid-snap. She didn't think he would lose it like this, and it left her both scared and intrigued. "Look, it's important we take care of James in a professional and respectful manner."

"It's hardly respectful that you have police traipsing through my set," Anciaux said. "You need us here to pay the mortgage on this place far more than we need some drama-fueled, nepotism-rife ranch."

"If that's what you think—"

She scowled at Wade, silencing him. This fight was on her, and she needed to make things right. "This is getting out of hand. We'll talk to the officers on scene and make a point of getting this situation handled as quickly as possible. If we do so quietly, which I think we can do—possibly without even the cast knowing more than they already do—you can resume shooting as early as eight a.m. Does that sound fair?"

The director gave her a look of disbelief. "I highly doubt you can get things wrapped up that quickly in this backwoods holler—or whatever redneck thing you call this uncultured map dot."

Wade flinched, and she could tell it was taking him every bit of his willpower not to reach out and touch the director. It made her feel vindicated in her anger with the man earlier—at least it wasn't just in her imagination how abrasive this man truly was—he was a porcupine in human form.

"We will." She sent Anciaux a saccharine-sweet smile. "And I'm sure, since you will have such a resoundingly positive experience with this security team, that you will continue to use them for your future projects. I would expect a contract sometime this week for the next six months. Yes?" She looked at Anciaux.

"I don't really see what's in it for me," the director countered. "You're paid to do a job. I shouldn't have to incentivize it to get you to do it."

She felt her lip curl. "If you don't agree to my terms, I can promise you that we can extend our investigation and make sure that we have the investigators pull you into their office for the full forty-eight-hour period in which they are allowed to hold you in order to conduct their interrogation."

Kim looked at her like Marie had thrown gas onto them and was waiting to light the match. Wade's hand moved to her lower back in support.

"You have until eight a.m. If we're forced to shut down because of this, then not only are you fired but so is this entire security team and we will be canceling our contract with the ranch," Anciaux said with a sneer. He turned with a flourish of the hand and stomped off, mumbling something to Kim.

She was nodding away in true minion form.

"Emily is going to be pissed," Wade said, running his hand over his face. "Gah."

"You're right—I am." Emily's voice pierced the air.

She turned toward the sound, and Emily was standing there, within striking distance. "Did you really think your little meltdown here wouldn't get everyone's attention?" Emily nearly growled.

"That guy had it coming. You didn't hear what he said," Wade countered.

"I don't care if he called me an upside-down leprechaun with piles. Do you just realize what you did to me?"

Marie tried not to smirk.

"And you…" Emily turned to her. "Since you have set foot on this ranch, don't think I haven't noticed that you have been at the center of far too many incidents. If you get into anymore issues, I will let you go. Consider yourself on probation."

Chapter Ten

There was nothing for Wade to do but get the heck out of Emily and her team's way—he'd forced their hands into rushing a crime scene, and he was wracked with guilt for losing his patience and putting everything in jeopardy. He had never been great at handling emotions, and until recently, he had been proud of his ability to push them down and force them into submission. Yet being here and around Marie had brought a number of things to the surface.

As they left, he felt as though he was going from one hot pot into the next. There were perpetual battles wherever he found himself, and he hated that he had gotten himself in this position. He had to distance himself from the family and the investigation, but that meant he was gambling being so close to Marie.

She had been lying to him. Everything in his entire body and every cell of his intuition was telling him that she wasn't to be trusted, and yet he was constantly being pulled to her and wanting to touch her. Even when he had gone toe to toe with Anciaux, he had needed to touch her back to feel grounded.

It was like she was his personal good-luck totem, but also the black cat in his path. It was just a good thing he had a thing for cats.

"I want to head up the mountain," he said, pointing up in the darkness in the general direction of the Clark Range.

Marie shot him a look. "It's four o'clock in the morning. Do you really think we're going to find anything out there in the middle of the night?"

He didn't dare tell her what he was really thinking—that he would rather spend a night in the woods with mountain lions and bears than be alone with her in his camper. The furry predators were far more predictable.

"It's fine." He didn't even bother to explain himself. He felt like a jerk being so cold, but on the other hand, he had to do his job—some boundaries were there for a reason and required reinforcement.

She let out a long exhale. "I don't know about you, but I'm getting tired."

"You can catch a nap. It's a bit of a drive to where I want to go."

They pulled onto a dirt road on the outskirts of the ranch that led in the direction of the mountains that hovered around them in the moonlight. The truck bumped along the road, the tires crunching on the dirt and gravel as they slowly made their way.

It didn't take long before Marie's chest started to rise and fall with the soothing rhythm of sleep.

Though he shouldn't have been relieved, he was glad that she had fallen into the grips of rest. It gave him a chance to think about everything he wanted to do and how he was going to learn more about her and her motives. There were several things he knew for sure: She wasn't here by some random coincidence. Though she couldn't have been the one to kill James, he couldn't discount the possibility that she still had something to do with his death. And he couldn't help the attraction he felt for her even though he was playing with fire.

He looked over at her as the sun started to rise on the horizon. The soft glow picked up the copper red tones of blond in her hair and the shimmer of eyeshadow that had settled into the creases of her eyelids. She was undeniably sexy and so different from any other woman he had ever been with. If it wasn't for the myriad of red flags she presented, he could have easily fallen for her straight-to-the-point attitude and desire for adventure.

They had so many things in common—from the way she seemed to run toward chaos to the light in her eyes when she'd been in the fray with the director.

He would never understand how his sister, Scarlett, loved that world of acting and heavily egotistic coworkers and bosses. Then again, as he thought about it, perhaps her world was more similar to his than he would have liked to admit. He dealt with high-level dignitaries who had far worse egos than the pissant Anciaux.

The biggest difference between him and Scarlett was the fact that he liked to live his life in the background and out of the spotlight—much like Marie.

She had said she had worked as a beat cop in Arlington, but there were so many idiosyncrasies about her that he wasn't sure he believed her. Sure, she might have been a cop at one time or another, thanks to the way she seemed to be constantly searching the areas around her.

There were a lot of other jobs that were

similar to law enforcement which would have led to her acting as she did, his being one of them. It wasn't common for a woman to be a military contractor, however. It wasn't a job that lent itself to gender diversity due to the global climate and attitude toward women. There were many countries in which she couldn't have set foot, at least without a man present, if she were to go in public.

For him, he didn't have to worry about those kind of things. He could come and go and blend into the culture as much as his physique and costuming would allow. What's more, Americans were everywhere and unless he was in a small town, his presence didn't always draw scrutiny. He couldn't say the same for an American woman.

In Afghanistan, for example, one of the VIPs he had worked with, the former Secretary of Defense for the United States, had gone incognito in hopes of better understanding the pressures and conflicts that they faced. Even when she was with a team of contractors and they were going low-pro, there were always people watching.

It had been one of his most hated and stressful assignments. How that woman had made it out alive was still a mystery. She'd looked and acted the part of an Afghan woman, from her head covering to her adherence to cultural rules and mores, but she was still a woman in public. There was no possibility that anyone knew who she was, and he could have only imagined how dangerous situation would have been had they known what a powerful woman they'd had in their area.

All that being said, there were women who worked in military contracting for the UN and private groups through them. They could go into situations and private residences in ways that he, and other men, couldn't. Meeting one of these women was like meeting a ghost. He wasn't even sure they really existed beyond rumor.

Yet instinct told him that he might well be in the presence of a Casper.

He looked over at her, and her eyes were fluttering with REM sleep.

If she was a contractor, it would have helped to make sense why James had been carrying a picture of her in his backpack. Well, maybe. It wasn't unheard of for one contracting group to be in contact with another, at least at a leadership level. They regularly competed for contracts from the United Nations and other well-heeled countries and organizations. In many situations, money was the ultimate judge of not only which side prevailed in a fight but which battles were even remembered.

If she was with a fellow group, or even with his own and he just wasn't aware of her within the Vaquero organization, it still left the question of why she would have come to the ranch. Was the tie between her and James? He couldn't help but wonder if she knew more about why James had been there than she admitted.

If she wished him harm, which was a possibility, she could have killed them by now. So at least, he could have a modicum of solace in the fact he was still breathing.

The only other reason he could think of why someone from a contracting group would attempt to infiltrate his life was if they were trying to gather information.

His stomach tightened. *That was it.* She was his own personal spy.

Sure, he could be wrong, but he doubted it. She wasn't like anyone else he'd ever met outside of the world of contracting and war.

In addition to those who worked in contracting, there were ancillary positions she could have also held. He regularly worked with CIA operatives and MI5. Regardless of who her bosses were, the end result was the same: She was here to dig into him and learn something.

Perhaps that was what James had been here to warn him about. He was trying to tell Wade that there was a ghost in their midst. It would hardly have been the first time that he had found himself under some sort of investigation, but this definitely was the most intense period. No one had ever followed him back to the United States, or outside of a country where a particular incident had taken place. Usually, he was under investigation by people within his own group to make sure that they were complying with international laws and rules of engagement, but truth be told those laws were hard to enforce and often ignored.

He made every effort to comply with the laws. It made for an easier and more professional experience in the field. And long term, it reduced incidents like that which he was currently facing.

James had worked with him for about six months in Iraq and Afghanistan, moving VIP and assets from one location to the next, making sure that no matter what their asset was—from human to currency—it remained undetected and safe.

That was until that last mission in Hawija.

Wade had been team leader that day. It had been his responsibility to make sure that his team of contractors made a smooth pickup and dropped off their asset to their target location. He didn't always know what they were moving. Often he never even saw anything beyond boxes, bins, or steel containers being loaded into one of the vehicles in their caravan.

On that particular day, he had seen five large steel containers being loaded by a front-end loader into a line of low-profile white Toyota pickups, similar to that which had run into the restaurant upon his arrival to Montana and could be seen anywhere.

He had to admit how much he hated those pickups.

In Hawija, they'd had to make sure their vehicles were not only bulletproof and IED-ready, but they had run-flat tires and souped-up suspension for carrying additional weight at possible high speeds.

The logistics team had taken care of everything, and it was on him and his team to just take the boxes from point A to B.

From there they had left the FOB and headed to their pickup location, loaded the Toyotas, and headed off to point B.

They were only thirty minutes out when

they had been hit. It was as if someone had been set up and waiting for the town as they had been moving north to Kirkuk. He spent so many nights wondering if they had been set up and, if they had, who had divulged their location and operational procedure.

Perhaps that was why everything was happening now. If James or Marie had been the one to throw his teammates and group under the bus for personal gain, that would explain their coming here.

Before he could face things head on with Marie, if his assumptions were right, he'd need to find out the truth about her.

He'd also need to know if his assumptions about the situation were correct. He'd like to think he wasn't oblivious or paranoid. Being aware of his surroundings and the people around him was a critical aspect of his job, and when he failed it resulted in events like that in Hawija—people that were important to him ended up getting hurt.

Now he just needed to find out if Marie was one of the people he had to worry about getting hurt or one of the ones who posed a threat to his family and friends.

The roads leading to the area behind the ranch and up the mountain were filled with ruts, and it took longer for him to get to the place he'd had in mind. It had been years since he'd been up in these hills, but some things hadn't changed. The ponderosa pine still stood tall like sentinels on the range.

When he'd been in high school there was a particular granite outcrop where he had loved to take his dates and look at the stars. It was one of the few locations that had a clear view of the ranch, without anyone being able to see them from below.

If he had been the sniper tasked with shooting James, it would have been the location he would have chosen. Thanks to global mapping and the ease of technology, he had a feeling it was one of just a couple places that he'd have to look to find more information about James's death.

The sun was just cresting the top of the mountain as he pulled to a stop at the trail that led to the rock outcrop. Marie was not stirring, and he watched her sleep for a moment. It wouldn't take much in a moment like this to get into her phone and dig around. However, even as un-techy as he was, he knew that she was likely to have the kind that snapped a picture anytime anyone but her tried to access the device. It wouldn't take long for her to figure out he'd been invading her privacy.

He had to find some other way for answers.

Again, he came back to the fact she hadn't harmed him…yet.

He slipped out of the pickup and gently closed the door, making sure not to shake the pickup as he moved. He didn't need her to go where he was going, and he hadn't seen another vehicle or evidence of anyone on the mountain since he'd been driving. He could safely say that if the shooter had been up here, they hadn't gotten there through that particular access road.

As he hiked along the thin, rocky trail, he thought about the other ways to get to this area. There was one logging road that headed this direction from the southwest or a person could have hiked up from an access point on the river. It would have been a heck of a hike but not impossible.

That was how he would have accessed the point undetected. After that, for a sniper once they were in a location, set up, and concealed, it became a waiting game. James had made himself an easy target.

Coming to the ranch just to tell him about

this woman, Marie, certainly it wasn't enough of a reason to be murdered.

What was he missing?

The pine needles on the trail crunched under his feet. He searched the ground for tracks, but thanks to the pine needles and gravel that littered the path, it was hard to detect what was animal and what was possibly made by humans. Something had traveled through. There were areas of kicked-up dirt and broken sticks, but it could have been anything from a bear to a bobcat that had traveled through in the night or early morning hours before he'd arrived. They could have even come through yesterday, as there had been no major weather for wind to disturb the trail.

The last time he'd been up here it was the night of his senior prom, in the early morning hours, after he and his beautiful date, Heather, had spent the night dancing and partying with friends. Each told their parents they were spending the night with friends, but in the end, they had spent the night under the stars telling each other secrets. It had been one of the purest nights of love and intimacy that he'd had in his life.

With the thought, he hated that he was now

coming here to investigate the area in a possible murder of a friend. Yet long ago he had learned that nothing could be sacred in this life. Everything the person held dear or special could be taken away.

Then again, perhaps it was the memories that mattered the most. It was those moments in time that had made him the man he was, for good or bad.

As he made his way out of the timber and to the outcrop of granite, he had a sinking sensation that his assumption had been right. There on the main point, the dirt had been packed down and a silver-colored casing from a rifle round littered the ground.

Whoever made the shot on James hadn't thought someone would come up here, or they would never have left their brass. He didn't want to touch the item, out of fear that it held possible answers to the shooting. He'd have to get Emily and her team up here to conduct a fingerprint analysis .

He didn't know a lot about what the investigation team did, but he did know that in his line of work one of the main sources of fingerprints was the brass from guns. The person usually had to touch them in order to load their weapon. Sure, there were ways around it, and if a person was aware that they were possibly going to be searched for, they could take measures to prevent leaving prints. But based on the sniper's indifference to being found here, he held hope.

There were also the snipers and shooters who didn't care about leaving prints behind, because they knew that there was nothing to be found even if they were attained. Unfortunately, the hubris was well founded and it matched the MO of this shooter, so far as he could tell.

He wouldn't know anything for sure until Emily got up here and they did their full analysis and investigation. He squatted down and took a picture of the casing with his phone. He enlarged it so he could read the caliber, .308.

It was interesting that the shooter had chosen to use a nickel casing. It told him something else: This person understood ballistics and the impact of temperature on weaponry. Nickel rounds could be bought over the counter at most gun stores, but they were often about two to three times more expensive and not used by what he would consider everyday shooters.

It wouldn't surprise him if this person actually loaded their own ammo. Which, if that was the case, the ballistics on this would be easier if they found the bullet embedded in James's body or somewhere else. If they got their hands on the gun, all it would take would be a couple hours in the lab and they could confirm whether or not the weapon was used in the shooting.

Before they could do that, though, they'd have to figure out who would have wanted to pull the trigger.

He thought back to the steel boxes they had been moving with the Toyota Hiluxes. He hadn't known what was in them, only that they were very heavy. He had also not been told who'd hired their company to move the material. As for who would have wanted to attack them and stolen it, it was up for debate.

He sent the picture he'd taken of the spent brass, the coordinates of the location, and a text with his thoughts about a possible sniper to Emily. She texted him back within seconds.

I don't know what you're doing up there. If you had an idea of where we could find the shooter, you should have told me directly. I don't need you out there disturbing a possible crime scene. Leave it now. I'll send an officer.

He wasn't surprised that she wasn't pleased. He couldn't find it within himself to tell her that he'd found this place on a hunch. It wouldn't look good for him, and he was clearly already walking on eggshells with his sister-in-law.

He sent a quick text in response.

The shooter may have been loading his own ammo. Make sure to run a metal detector on the scene if X-ray doesn't show bullet or fragments within James's remains.

He was sure he didn't have to tell her how to do his job, but he couldn't help himself.

Thanks.

His phone dinged again with a second message.

Don't get yourself shot. Go home.

He took a series of photographs of the area, making sure not to disturb anything.

Though he was aware he should head back to the pickup and Marie, curiosity beckoned him. He picked his way carefully down the rock outcrop looking for anything that would provide more clues to the identity of the shooter.

Near the bottom of the small cliff, the rocks grew sharper and more dangerous as the outcrop turned from granite to shale. Sticking up from one of the darker purplish-hued rocks was a smudge of something wet.

Moving closer, he could make out what appeared to be blood, as if someone had grabbed the edge of the stone and cut their hand while moving through the debris. The blood had started to dry around the edges of the print, which was in a crescent shape, like that of the base of a person's palm.

He took a quick pic and sent it to Emily along with the coordinates of the find.

Her response was almost immediate:

GO. HOME.

He was so close to getting answers—the shooter was closer than he anticipated. The blood was still wet, and from the direction of the palmprint on the rock, it looked like the person had been going downhill. It made him wonder if the sound of their vehicle had actually surprised the person and they had scurried from their hide.

His senses tingled, telling him that he was on to something. It would make sense that the shooter had left their casing and had cut their hand. They'd been in a hurry.

There were only so many places a person could safely cross the river if they were hiking out of this location. He and Marie would have to get to one of those crossings before they did, or he'd never have a chance of finding them.

From above him on the mountain, Marie's voice echoed down. "Are you okay?"

"Yeah. Fine." He was far from all right, but for the first time since the shooting he felt like he was in control. If they played this smart, he could find much needed answers.

Chapter Eleven

Marie made her way down the hillside, carefully picking her way through the jagged rocks and boulders. She wiped the sleep from her eyes, but she still felt as though she was slogging through the swamps of drowsiness.

Unfortunately, she was used to this power-nap lifestyle, and she hated and loved it equally. On one hand, it reminded her of the Einstein sleep pattern for maximum efficiency. And little sleep meant less of a chance for dreaming—her dreams always had a way of turning into nightmares.

"You look exhausted," Wade said as she caught up to him at the bottom of the scree field near the rocky overhang.

It was a pretty area, but she wasn't sure exactly what had brought them to this location.

Wade had been acting so strangely around her. Was it possible he had brought her there to make her disappear?

Her skin prickled with fear.

If he had figured out who she was and why she was there, and if he did play a role in the theft, then it would have been to his benefit to make her disappear. It would be the perfect way to hide her body—they weren't that far from Glacier National Park, a place notorious for grizzlies, wolves, mountain lions, and an abundance of scavengers that could quickly make a body disappear.

If she was found, it would be unlikely that her body would provide any answers as to what had happened to cause her death—and Wade would walk free with the money from his raid.

No, she thought. *He cares about me.*

Or did he?

He had helped her get the security position on the set, and he had been a constant presence since she had stepped foot on the ranch, but was that not because of a bond but rather because he was watching her?

There was only one way to find out, but she'd have to be careful.

"Wade." She spoke his name softly, the sounds like a caress, and she watched as his body seemed to tense.

"Yes?"

She moved beside him and put her hand on his arm. "I want you to know how much I appreciate you letting me tag along with you."

"Did I really have a choice?" From the stoic look on his face, she couldn't decide whether or not he was being serious or teasing her, but she had a feeling it was the latter.

"If you don't want me to be here, I can just get back on the road." She thumbed in the direction of the ranch truck that was sitting on the logging road above. "You just need to take me back, and I'll get my pickup and head out."

She didn't want to leave, not in the slightest, and she would have been lying if she had tried to say it was just because of her assignment. There was something about the handsome cowboy that she had come to truly appreciate. And though she couldn't think about having a relationship with him—or anyone, thanks to her job—if she could, he would have been her first choice.

If nothing else, if she was close to him, she could live in her own fantasy world and pretend there could be a future for the limited time they were together.

He sighed, and he ran his hands over his face, pulling at his skin with frustration.

"Look, you need to tell me who you really are and why you are at the ranch."

She took a step back. He was nothing, if not direct. "I'm Marie Costa."

"Is that your real name?"

"Why would you think it wasn't?" She scowled, trying to play it as innocently as possible as she weighed whether to tell him some version of the truth.

"Look, I found a picture of you and some other women in James's things. I need to know why he would have been keyed in on you and then you suddenly show up at the ranch."

His hand twitched as though he was thinking about reaching for a weapon.

"You don't need to do that," she said, motioning toward his hand. "I'm not your enemy."

"Then tell me who the hell you are. Now. No more games." He dropped his hand to his side, but his right hovered over what must have been a gun inside his waistband.

She had always thought he was carrying, but she hadn't really been concerned until now. "I'm like you."

He shot her a look that told her that wasn't nearly enough of an acceptable answer.

"I work for a group like you."

"They sent you here to spy on me? Or on James?"

"Yes." She tried to control the fear that was starting to build up within her. If he thought he could kill her without her putting up a fight, he was dead wrong.

"Who?"

"I was supposed to look into you. James was just a bennie." She shrugged.

"What were you digging into us about?"

The way his voice changed pitch made her think he already knew exactly why she would have been investigating him. "Hawija. How long had you been planning the attack?"

"What in the hell are you talking about? I had nothing to do with the attack. I was there, doing my job and protecting the caravan. Do you really think I'd risk my job, my honor, and my integrity just to take a gamble on something we'd been hired to protect?"

"I think people would do anything for the right amount of money. We just have to find what motivates a person, and in my position, I've found I can get them to do pretty much whatever I want—even kill."

"Then you're the one who should be under investigation, not me." He turned away from her, anger radiating from him.

She touched his arm, but he jerked away from her touch. The rejection stung more than she would have expected. "Wade," she said his name like it was an olive branch. "I'm sorry. You know how it is to be sent to do a job. How do you think it looked when I walked up on the situation with James's shooting?"

He glowered at her. "Did you tell your bosses I had something to do with that? You know I didn't. You've even said—"

"I haven't told them anything." She put her hands up in surrender. "I won't until I have all the answers."

Some of the anger seemed to drift from him. "You still haven't revealed the question."

"I was sent here to find out what you know about the attack and what role you played."

"I promise you I had nothing to do with what went down."

Marie wanted to believe him, but it was hard given everything she had learned before she had come to the ranch. "If you didn't come here, why were your fingerprints found on the empty shipping containers?"

"What?" His eyes were wide with shock. "I never touched the containers. I barely ever saw them. In fact, I think the only time I saw one of them was when it was being loaded onto the Hilux. The only reason I remember is that they had put in airbag suspension. It was the first time I'd seen something like that in person. I thought it was strange."

"Why would that have been strange?" she pressed.

"Airbag suspension, put in aftermarket, is highly unusual for those trucks. It was an indication that whatever it was we were protecting had serious weight."

"Did you know what you were tasked with protecting in that transport?"

He shook his head. "All I knew, or know, was that it was heavy."

She studied him, looking for the rapid blinking or flickering gaze that would give away a lie, but she found nothing to indicate he was trying to falsify his statement. "You do know how it looks that only you and two others made it out of that attack alive? And then you disappeared into the wilds of Montana?"

"Ha. Is that what you think? I robbed the caravan and ran?" He paused. "Is that what the UN thinks, or is it the CIA?"

"I work for a group like yours."

He nodded, and this time he was the one studying her. She could tell he wanted to ask her about her affiliation. "Mark, Andrew, and Shawn were also there," he continued, "but I don't think any of them would have wanted to get wrapped up in a heist. Do you have people investigating them as well?"

"Mark and Andrew didn't make it out of Iraq. They were killed the day you flew out."

The color drained from his face. "That's not possible. That means only Shawn and I are alive from our original team."

"And now you know why I'm a little leery about your involvement. It's strange that you are still standing." What she couldn't wrap her head around was the fact that James had been carrying a picture of her. How had he gotten the information that she had been sent there? "Can I see the picture you were telling me about, from James's tent?"

He reached into his back pocket but then stopped. "If we are going to have any chance at getting our hands on James's shooter, then we need to get moving."

"Why don't you want to show me?"

"You have to respect that I'm going to be leery. I need to look into your story as much as you need to look into mine." He stuffed his hand into his pocket. "If you check out, I'll show you."

"I'll check out."

"As will I," he said.

"If that's the case, then it is in our best interest to keep you protected and to find out who was really behind the heist—I have a feeling you may have more answers about what happened than what you think."

He stopped and turned from the trail ahead and peered back at her over his shoulder, and in the morning light he looked tired but so unexpectedly sexy that it made her chest tighten. She had no idea what came over her, and she tried to push down the feelings. Just because she had risked her career in telling him her truth didn't mean that they were any closer to actually being true friends—for the moment, they were merely allies.

Chapter Twelve

Nightmares became even more terrifying when they turned into reality. As Wade picked his way down the mountainside and toward the river crossing, he took out his phone and texted Emily to let her know they were tracking the possible shooter.

He studied the partial track, complete with the diamond-shaped bottom consistent with many brands of hiking boots. If he kept his eyes peeled, perhaps he would be able to pick up a full track, one that held the brand name or size. For now, he was happy to just find the occasion heel print.

From the size alone, it was impossible to decipher if the person wearing the boot was a man or woman, but from the pigeon-toed way they walked, he leaned toward a male. And that would only be because he had seen more than a few men who walked with their toes pointed in.

His mind went to Shawn Anchors, the man who had been on his team—and the only other one who was still standing. He had walked with a slight pigeon-toed gait, and he had always been the one to run tech for his team.

If anyone on his former Vaquero Team was capable of getting the intel in advance and setting up a hit, it would be Shawn. The man could do anything with a computer or a cell phone if he was just given time. Once, they had needed to find a kidnapped son of a Danish diplomat using only the signal given off by their smartwatch. It had taken Shawn a couple of hours, but using satellites, and a variety of tech that Wade never understood, he had managed to give them a two-block radius of the eleven-year-old boy. The kid had been back in his parents' arms by the next day.

The last time he had heard anything about Shawn, he had been living in Austin, hitting the music festivals and packing as much living into his days as he could before he returned to his job in the sandbox.

"You said your people are looking into Shawn as well?" he asked, keeping his voice low though he doubted they were close to the person they were tracking.

Marie moved beside him on the trail. "Yes, why?"

"Have you had any luck in locating him?"

"Oddly enough, I think we were going down the same rabbit hole." She looked down at the phone she held in her hand. "I contacted my captain. He said the contractor they have looking into him hasn't had any luck. Recently, the contractor disappeared. They last checked in near Salt Lake City."

"When Shawn left the country with me, he said he was going to go home to Austin for a bit."

She tapped away on her phone, and a moment later a text popped up on the screen in response. "Yeah. That's where they started. No luck. His family stated they hadn't even seen him since he'd initially deployed."

There was a chance Shawn had been waylaid on his journey home. They had split up mid-transfer in Amsterdam. The guy could have changed his mind, or he could have made any number of choices that had resulted in him not reaching his proposed final destination.

Though Wade knew it was unlikely he would get a response, he took out his phone and sent Shawn a text. They continued walking down the trail. He kept looking at his phone and hoped something would pop up on the screen from Shawn. No answer came.

"Salt Lake is just a stopover for most people who are driving up to Montana. At least, if they're coming from the south." Wade stuffed his phone back into his pocket. "I wonder if he and James had been in contact and maybe he was on his way up here as well."

Marie nodded. "It's definitely a possibility. It's also a possibility that he is as dead as James."

That had to mean someone was gunning for him. Someone was afraid of what he had seen and experienced that day in Iraq. He did a mental check of everything he could remember from that particular event, but nothing new came to mind. Until the attack, everything had been pretty cookie cutter and standard operating procedure. "Maybe it's not such a smart idea that we're trying to chase down this shooter. If this person is trying to get a sight line on me, then me getting closer to them is not perhaps the smartest move."

"From what I can tell, there are not a lot of open locations where the shooter could set up an ambush. That is, unless they double back on this and go up the mountain again." Marie pointed in the direction of their parked truck up on the hillside. "I don't know about you, but I'm not looking forward to trying to hike back up that hill. Down is bad enough."

He slipped slightly on the loose gravel of the trail as they descended a steep section. He reached out in an attempt to take hold of something to steady his balance, but as he moved, his hand moved against something wet.

He gazed over at the blood that was sticky on the rock, just like it had been above, however this blood seemed fresher and there were no dried edges around the crescent shape of the person's palm print. They were gaining ground, or perhaps they were getting entirely too close.

He wasn't worried about a gun fight. It wasn't the first time in his life he felt like he was about to face the firing squad. And just like every time before, he felt a sense of empowerment and pride that he wasn't afraid. In fact, he felt confident that his expertise in the field would prove to be a major benefit.

He could take down just about anyone.

"We have another print," he said to Marie, pointing it the witness. "If something happens and we draw fire, how comfortable are you having my six?"

He could feel that she wanted to say something snarky, but she withheld. "It feels like since the moment I've gotten on the ranch, that's all we've been doing. If you think anything has changed, you're sorely mistaken."

"I hope you know you can trust me. I really am on your side," she said, sounding almost like she was at war with herself.

"I also understand that you have a job to do," he countered.

She gave him a curt nod. "I do." Her hand instinctively moved to her phone.

"Did your boss text you, ask where you were at in your investigation?"

She peered down at the palm print.

"I hope you told them that you know I'm not the one behind the robbery."

"Technically it was a theft," she quietly corrected him. "And yes, I did."

"I hope your word carries weight and you didn't just put a target on your back, too." He couldn't help the creeping fear that grew within him that she had done just that. If she had been working under him and their target was in a situation like his, he would have had one heck of a time believing that their target was innocent.

He had to hope against all hopes that her bosses were honorable people.

Right now, he found himself wondering if his bosses at the Vaquero Group were possibly the ones who had done him wrong. In some ways, it made sense—they could have stolen the entire shipment and pinned it on him. Take him out, and they would be covered. Then again, the people or governments who hired their company to do the jobs would be out for reparation. They wouldn't be happy until they had their losses recovered.

If the Vaquero owner or leaders were behind this, killing the team members wouldn't completely solve their problems. Every one of them would be out of business, and then they would have to disappear. Plus, it would have taken at least three people to pull off the hit. Each truck required a driver. The more people, the more the money would be divided, and that was to say nothing about the bribes it would have taken to get the money safely out of the country undetected.

Add to that the fact someone would have to turn around and sell the gold, or turn it into cash without drawing scrutiny—especially if their names and faces were on international watch lists. Though he knew for a fact there were plenty of dark-web types who would be more than happy to take the bars and melt them down—for a price.

He had only ever wanted to do his job. It irritated him to no end that this is now where he found himself after doing all he could to make sure everyone in his life understood he was, and would always be, an honorable man.

There was the sound of scattering rocks from farther down the mountain, and it drew Wade's attention from his torturous thoughts.

He stood still, listening. There was the sound of a woman's voice, but he couldn't quite make out what they were saying. What he did know was that if the person's voice was carrying up from the bottom of the mountain, theirs had to be carrying down as well. They'd have to be very quiet in hopes that the person they were tracking wasn't aware they were close on their heels.

He moved slower, making every effort not to disturb a single stone as they picked their way down the steep hillside. It was likely the woman had slipped, possibly pulled off balance thanks to the rifle and pack she was likely carrying. If she was hurt and rocking, it made sense that they had caught up to her.

He couldn't let this opportunity slip through

his fingers. He had to get his hands on James's killer. He needed the answers. And he needed to clear his name. The only way to do that would be to find whoever had pulled that trigger.

He motioned back to Marie, who was a few dozen yards up the mountain from him. She had paused and was looking at something, but he couldn't make out what she was studying.

He sent her a hand signal asking if she was okay. She responded by pointing at the ground where she was looking. He watched as she took out her phone and snapped the picture and motioned for him to take out his phone.

He did as she requested, and a moment later a photo of two sets of tracks, neither being his, appeared on the ground near where he had just moved down the mountain.

He wasn't sure how he had missed them. The marks from each of the tracks were nearly complete, as if the hikers had stepped into a slightly muddy area and it had captured their footsteps. The one boot was significantly larger than the other, indicating that they likely had a male and a female in front of them.

He took a long breath, re-centering himself and shifting his mindset. If there were two, that meant it must have been the sniper and their spotter up on the point and not just a single person.

If anything, he should have thought about that before. It wasn't unheard of for snipers to work alone, but the best usually worked as a part of a team. And if they were part of a team, they probably had other members waiting to extract them from the location. If that was the case, he and Marie were walking into a firestorm. The idiom bringing a knife to a gunfight came to mind.

They weren't just dealing with an angry operative who was working rogue or seeking revenge.

He considered turning back and going up the mountain to the truck, but if they let this shooter go, they would never know who was gunning for them. Their lives, particularly his, were at serious risk.

No matter how much the odds were stacked against them, he couldn't go down without a fight. If someone wanted to pin this heist on him, they weren't going to get away with it that easily.

He slipped his phone back into his pocket as he thought about the topography of the land below. From this point it wasn't much farther until they reached the river. The river slowed where the person would need to cross, and beyond that was a large open bank, which was normally flooded out in the early spring due to the runoff. He could catch them crossing the river. It would be the best time to get them in his sights.

The real question would be whether or not he could keep them alive long enough for them to talk and reveal what was going on. He needed a face to his enemy. There was no way he could win if he was fighting shadows.

If his assumptions were correct, the odds weren't in his favor.

Marie's features darkened and she scowled as she moved down the trail toward him. She had to have been as concerned with the new information as he was. She was a contractor; she had to have known the obstacles they would face.

One aspect he hadn't considered was the fact he did have her. If push came to shove, at least he wasn't alone. It also meant he would have to trust that she truly was on his side. And if this situation had ingrained anything in him it was that he didn't know anyone's true motives.

There was the scattering of stones as Marie started to slide toward him. She grappled around the area, reaching for a branch or outcrop that would stop her fall, but before she could grasp anything she had slipped nearly to him. He grabbed at her as rocks and debris rolled over his feet and went crashing down the mountain.

There went their element of surprise, and with it went any advantage they held.

The team below had to know they were being tracked.

He lifted Marie to her feet. Her face was covered in a fine layer of dust, and her hands were covered in scrapes and chunks of rocks were embedded in her palms where she had clawed for a handhold.

"Are you okay?"

"I… I'm sorry I lost my footing," she stammered, gesturing up the mountain. Small stones were still cascading down the hill.

"Are you hurt anywhere?" He looked her over as she picked at the gravel stuck in her skin.

"Only my ego is hurt." She looked down the mountain in horror. "Do you think they heard that?"

He wiped a bit of dirt from her cheek. "I think everyone in the entire Flathead Valley heard that."

Overhead there as the sound of a helicopter's blades chopping through the air. They stared up at the sky as the blue aircraft brushed low over the tops of the trees to the right and swooped down toward the valley. It moved out of sight, but he could hear it hover near the river.

It lifted straight up into the air, and there was a blonde woman climbing up a rope ladder toward the open side door of the bird. He couldn't make out her face, only her long hair and the gun strapped to her pack as she slipped inside.

The helicopter disappeared into the distance as quickly as it had come.

They had lost their sniper.

Chapter Thirteen

It was impossible to make up for the mistake Marie had just made, and no amount of apologizing was going to get them close to the shooter ever again—at least not when they were the ones doing the hunting. Now they were going to go back to being stalked and hunted like prey.

Wade sat down on the ground and put his arms on his knees and dropped his head, making his look even more despondent than she felt.

She didn't know what to do next. They were at least a mile downhill from his truck. Now it almost had to be quicker to go to the river and ford across the water to the ranch instead of trying to make the trek back up. No matter what they did, she would not be able to stop chastising herself for her blunder.

Then she remembered why she had stopped

before the fall. "Did you see anyone else in that helo?"

Wade glanced up at her. The way he looked at her made her want to curl up into a ball and disappear. "No."

"I didn't, either." She smiled as the realization struck her. "There is still another person out here."

His eyes widened slightly and then his frown disappeared. "Do you think?"

She nodded wildly. "There wasn't enough time for the bird to pick up two people—to say nothing about the size of the helicopter itself. That was a small one."

She didn't know a whole lot about helicopters other than having ridden them a few times when she had been traveling around countries for her job. They were fast and effective, but they were notorious for their falling from the sky—with or without gunfire or attacks.

It was not one of her favorite ways to travel, but the views from the birds were beautiful and the experiences always made her heart race. Though she knew it wasn't likely, she always felt like she was one second away from disaster inside; and being that hair's breadth from danger was one of the few things that really made her feel like she was human.

Wade stood up, brushing off the seat of his pants. "You're right. We need to keep moving. There may be someone else down there. Maybe the team had to make a split-second decision on who to extract. Regardless, this is our only chance."

Her feet were shaky from the slip, but she tried her best to keep her footing and not make the same mistake she had before. It didn't take much long at their new pace to make it to the bottom of the mountain.

She found the spot in the grass that the woman had paced while waiting for the helicopter, and then her footprints disappeared. The larger prints, the one she assumed was a male's, moved west toward the river. Wade took point, and she hurried behind him in hopes that at least they could get eyes on the man.

On the flat land leading to the river, the ground grew softer and the world around them turned from a rocky hillside with pines into a riparian zone complete with cottonwood trees and the scratching clawlike branches of hawthorn and willow bushes.

A thorn tore across her cheek, but she barely noticed as she tried to control her breathing. They were so close—she could feel it. All they had to do was keep pushing forward and they could get their hands on the man they were searching for.

She pushed through the next bush, and the twig in front of her swung back and slapped her on the face. "Son of a…" she mumbled.

Wade turned and looked back at her. He mouthed the word *Sorry* for letting go of the branch, but she waved him off. It wouldn't have been so bad if only she had been paying attention.

In an attempt to stop herself from being whipped again behind Wade, she rushed to catch up, and she moved around him on the right.

A pair of arms moved around her, and a man's hand clamped over her mouth. She tried to scream as she threw her head back, attempting to hit her attacker in the face with the crown of her skull. She connected with the person's shoulder, but the man's grip didn't lighten.

"Be quiet. I don't know who else is out here," the man whispered into her ear. "You already ran off my main target. I don't need you getting me shot, too."

She turned and tried to see his face, but the man held her.

"I'm assuming Wade knows he's a target?" the man asked.

Marie shook her head, and the man lessened his grip.

"No screaming." He let her turn around to face him.

The man looked familiar. There was a darkness in his brown eyes she could have sworn she had seen somewhere before, and his dark brown hair was shaggy and down around his ears even though it was tucked under a knit black cap that was far too warm for the autumn heat.

"Who are you? What do you want?"

The man stared at her face. "I could ask you the same."

"I'm helping Wade track *you* and your sniper. If he catches you, he is going to kill you."

The man laughed, the kind where only one side of his upper lip turned up and it made him look devilish. "You don't know him like I do. You spend that much time in the sandbox with someone, you tend to bond. But I've been wrong before." The man shrugged. "If he shoots me, you can have my watch." He lifted his wrist like the plastic thing on his wrist was something worthy of praise.

"Shawn?" She stared at him, looking for the man she had only seen in pictures during her briefing for this assignment.

"The one and only."

"What are you doing here? Why were you helping the sniper?"

There was the sound of Wade moving toward them in the bushes. "Marie, where are you?" he asked, his voice a frantic, hoarse whisper.

"She's here, Wade."

He punched through the bushes, his gun raised, and he pointed it squarely at Shawn's chest. As he saw the man, Wade lowered his weapon. "Dude. What in the hell?" He sounded shocked and relieved at the same time.

Shawn moved around her and grabbed Wade in a brotherly hug complete with a hard slap on the back. "You have no idea how happy I am to find you alive, brother."

"What's going on? You didn't hurt my friend here, did you?" Wade chided, taking Marie gently by the arm and moving her beside him like a protective lover.

Her heart stuttered, but she tried to keep herself in check. It was only the adrenaline of the moment and the lack of sleep that was making her feel the way she was feeling. It had nothing do to with how warm Wade's hand felt against her skin.

He looked at her. "What happened to your face?" He scowled over at Shawn. "Tell me you didn't have a hand in this." His voice was steely.

Shawn appraised her as if he was seeing her for the first time. "Not from me, man."

She put her fingers on her cheek and drew them back, noticing the streaks of blood on her fingertips. "Oh, that's from the hike. The thorns."

Wade scowled, but Shawn looked over at him and gave him a slight raise of the brows. "Ha."

"Don't even start," Wade said, but Marie wasn't sure what he was referring to. If Shawn was somehow implying there was something going on between the two of them, he was dead wrong. "Did you get an ID on the shooter?"

Shawn shook his head. "I managed to get some pictures of her and the helo. I'm hoping to run them through the databases and see if I can pull some facial recognition matches or some *N*-numbers deets."

"Did the helo's numbers actually start with an *N*?" she asked.

Shawn nodded.

"Then at least we know it came out of the US. It wasn't a foreign bird." It didn't mean much, but it was something.

Finally, they were getting answers.

THE FACT THAT HIS teammate was standing in the middle of the Montana wilderness, just on the outskirts of his ranch and carrying a rifle slung over his shoulder shouldn't have surprised Wade, given everything that had been going on. Ever since he had set foot down on American soil his life had been turned upside down, and the one place in the US he had thought would be a safe haven had been the deadliest place of all.

As they forded the river and walked up to the road where Emily had a truck waiting for them, they talked about Shawn and how he had come to the ranch. His story had been much the same: He had found out he had been being tailed, but in his case, he'd lost his tail and hitched a ride from a semi driver out of Austin into Salt Lake City. From there, he'd borrowed a friend's car and made his way north. He hadn't been exactly sure where to find the ranch, but apparently when he'd said the name *Trapper*, they were infamous enough that he was pointed in the right direction.

"My only hope was that I made it here in time," he said as they made their way up the grassy slope and slipped between the barbed wire that protected the riverbank from the erosion caused by grazing cattle. "I knew none of us stood a chance if we fought alone."

"Did you talk to James?" Wade asked.

He nodded. "He was the one who had come up with the plan." He pulled out his phone and, opening it up, clicked on a picture. "Take a look at this." He handed the device over to Wade as Shawn helped Marie slip through the strands of the wire.

The picture was of the same three women James had been carrying a picture of in his bag—Marie and the two unnamed others. He handed the phone back. Wade reached into his pocket, hoping the paper hadn't gotten wet on their river crossing. Thankfully, it was dry.

"I've seen those pictures before." He handed Shawn the piece of paper.

Shawn unfolded the paper just as Marie stood up. She pushed back her hair, forcing the loose strands by her face to move behind her ear.

"Oh." She covered her mouth as she caught sight of the paper in Shawn's hands.

He moved it so she could see it better. "You haven't seen this before?" He sent Wade a questioning glance.

He answered with a slight shake of the head.

"No," Marie said, her voice almost breathless.

"Do you know any of these other women?" Shawn pressed.

"There are only a small number of women who work as contractors, as I'm sure you both know." She started. "It's more dangerous for us out there."

"That's not an answer," Shawn countered. "Or are you saying you do? Are they from your group?"

She pointed to the blonde in the center. "She works with me. We don't get along." Then she pointed to the brunette on the left. "As for her, I don't know her."

"Do you have the picture you took of the woman, Shawn?" Wade asked.

Shawn took out his phone and pulled up a picture of the sniper from his phone. The picture was blurry, obviously having been taken while they were both moving. The woman's blond hair was flying behind her as she ran.

The rifle on her back was unique though—at the top of the barrel was a suppressor.

"Do you have any pictures of her face?" Marie asked, not daring to touch his phone but moving her hand toward it.

"You can look. I tried to take a video, but you can tell we were both running. I did the best I could given the circumstances." Shawn motioned for Wade to flip through. "The girl was good."

Marie nodded. "The blonde on my team, Mallory, is good with guns. But I could say the same of everyone I work with."

"Is she sniper good?" Wade asked.

"We can all sit on the working end of a sniper rifle." She shrugged. "If we couldn't, my bosses wouldn't have hired us."

She was being a hard head. Not everyone on every team needed to be running and gunning. Each person had their own skillset, and usually they were so honed in that they kept to their lane. At least, that was the case with the Vaqueros. He hadn't worked for another group, so it was hard to say how others operated, but from what he'd heard—until now—he'd thought they mostly worked the same.

"Is your group specifically used for long-range killing?" Shawn asked.

"No. We just go where we are most needed. Our members are trained for whatever operations we are hired to perform. I'm sure your group is the same way. I mean, look at what you were hired to move," she said, waving toward them. "You weren't even given armored vehicles. They clearly weren't expecting you to have trouble."

"If they were expecting trouble, they would have rerouted our caravan or changed the dates and times of the hand offs," Shawn said. "As for what we were moving, it was like any other job—and I only found out after the fact about the gold."

"How did you find out?" Wade asked, the hairs on his neck raising, but he wasn't sure if it was because he felt as though he was in danger or if it was something else he couldn't quite put his finger on.

Shawn pointed at the woman in the photograph, the brunette. "Chrissy rolled up on me. Started asking all kinds of questions." He looked over at Marie almost as if he wanted to say something more, but her being there stopped him. "Then she disappeared."

Marie opened her mouth like she wanted to speak, but then she clamped her jaws shut.

"Did you play a role in her disappearance,

Shawn?" Wade asked, trying not to sound accusatorial in the slightest.

"She disappeared around Salt Lake. I figured she had gotten the information she needed from me and then hightailed it out of there."

Wade scowled. "What did you tell her that would have made her leave?"

Shawn shrugged. "Just what I told you. I don't know anything about what happened back there in Hawija, and I sure as hell didn't have anything to do with any missing gold. If I did, I wouldn't have been so dumb as to stick around. There wouldn't have been a soul on this planet who would have testified to ever seeing me again."

"Three hundred million in gold can solve a lot of problems," Marie offered.

"And let me tell you," Shawn said, waving at her, "it can create just as many—even if you are close to it. We get paid well in our jobs, but we didn't get paid enough to put up with the aftermath. That gold is cursed."

Chapter Fourteen

Back at the camper, after they had met up with Emily and the men had briefed her on what had taken place on the mountain, Marie was taking a shower and getting cleaned up. From inside the square bathroom, she could hear Shawn and Wade talking outside, just enough to make out each person's voice but not enough to actually make sense of what they were saying.

She cranked open the vent in the room, but even with it open, she still couldn't hear them well enough, and she cussed under her breath at her luck.

It felt good to get out of her wet clothes that smelled like the river and a day's worth of stress sweat. Thanks to the dirt crushed into her shirt and mixed with the oils from her body, she was probably going to have to just throw the thing away. It was never going to be white again, no matter how many times she tried to wash it.

She slipped into a clean set of pants and a white tank top with a light button-up over the top. She didn't bother to button it; it was too hot outside as the day wore on. Even with the air conditioning on inside the trailer, she could feel the heat radiating off the walls thanks to the pressing down of the midday sun outside.

The state was wild. This morning it had been almost cold, and now they were talking temperatures into the hundreds, possibly topping out at 107 degrees. Her thoughts moved to the days she had spent training out of country. The number one rule had always been to stay hydrated. No matter what was wrong with a person from a headache to a missing limb, it had become a joke that people would tell them to *drink some water—you'll feel better.*

Today was one of those days.

Thinking about it, she went to the fridge and took out an icy bottle, cracked it open, and chugged it down. It gave her an instant brain freeze, and she groaned as she touched her temple. That had been stupid.

Her phone pinged from the table behind her. Picking it up, she read the message from her boss at Falcon. The message from Corey was simple, but it made her heart stutter:

Status check.

That was unusual. However, she had reached out to him about Shawn. No doubt it had raised some questions back at the incident command center.

As much as she wanted to click off the screen and pretend she hadn't gotten the message, that wasn't how she operated, nor was she allowed to. Instead, she played out all the possible answers in her head before sending back what she felt was the perfect response:

Making progress.

She nodded her head as she hit Send, proud of herself and her quick thinking. Corey would be happy with that. Sure, she didn't have things completely wrapped up, but given all that she had been through since she'd arrived in Montana, she had to say she was doing pretty well.

Assets being returned?

He was speaking about the gold. That was the only real asset they were concerned with saving. Lives of their enemies were just collateral damage to Corey—he'd made that clear before she'd left.

No known location. Working. Will contact when information becomes available.

Her stomach ached as she read through the words of her last text. Corey wasn't going to be pleased. As it was, if the blonde in the helicopter was the one from the picture, Corey had already sent in other contractors from her team to get the job done.

One thing about it though: It just didn't make sense to her why Corey would want to use his contractors to shoot and kill James. James could have held information. Sure, they had the clearances to kill as required, but they were instructed to do it quietly and to hide after the fact. Killing James in the middle of a television set was hardly under the radar.

She wanted to ask Corey outright if he had sent in Mallory, the other blonde from the photo James had been carrying around. Yet it wasn't her place to ask those kinds of questions. Her boss gave her the information she was meant to have. Anything more than that and it was none of her business. If he had kept things a secret from her, then he had his reasons.

In the end, she was here to perform her duties to the best of her abilities—in this case it was to find out what Wade knew about the heist and recover the missing gold. So far, she had been getting answers. They were working on the gold.

If Corey had sent in Mallory with the task of taking out the team members… Well, the thought didn't sit right in her soul. She couldn't go down that line of thinking. There was nothing to prove it had been Mallory in the helicopter or hunkered down on the point and pulling the trigger.

She thought back to the nickel-plated casing the shooter had left behind. In her team, in the past, Marie had been the only one to use that special casing. She liked it for its ability to remain frost-free in cold climates and its smooth feed and extraction from the chamber, but as most of their work was done in temperate climates, the others weren't as concerned with the casings themselves.

There was a modicum of comfort in the tiny detail she recalled from her and Mallory's differences while training in the field. Marie didn't know if she could handle the thought of her team actively trying to kill the man she was becoming more and more attracted to.

Maybe that was her signal that she needed to text her boss and tell him it was time to be removed from the operation. It was so unlike her to allow her feelings to get in the way. Yet she was facing questions about where her fealty lay—to her duty or to her heart.

This was why she couldn't allow herself to feel. Emotions were dangerous.

The screen on her phone turned off.

There was no way the woman on the helicopter was Mallory. That was it. No. It had to have been someone else. She just needed to find out the woman's real identity and clear her friend.

But if it was and Corey wasn't telling her… it could mean she was in the sights.

No. Her boss liked her. They had a good relationship. They'd been working together for nearly seven years. In that time, they'd only been face-to-face a handful of times, but when they were it was clear that they were brethren. Honor was the code of their lifestyle. If word got out that he went against his own, the killers who served him were likely to commit mutiny.

Corey wouldn't play such a dangerous game.

There was a knock on the trailer door. "Mind if I come in?" Wade asked.

"You're good," she said, giving herself a quick check in the bathroom mirror to make sure her hair was in place before she walked over, unlocked the door, and pushed it open.

Wade was standing there, sweat beading on his temples and staining the neck and pits of his shirt.

"The shower is ready for you," she said, nudging her chin in the direction of his shirt as he stepped up and inside the camper, closing the door behind him.

"Are you saying I smell?" he teased her.

It caught her a touch off guard, but she was glad that the softness in their friendship had returned. She hated the thought of him not trusting her, regardless of how well founded. If he only knew how she was feeling, he would never question a thing about her intentions with him. He was her unintentional weakness.

Yes, she definitely needed to get out of Montana.

"Yep," she teased back, making a cute scrunchy face and then sticking out her tongue. She flopped down onto the couch and lounged back.

"Just make yourself comfortable. You know, you made the whole trailer shake. Shawn is going to think we are in here doing *things*." A faint blush rose on his already heat-reddened cheeks.

She hadn't thought of that, and she could feel the blush rise on her face, too. "Oh." She giggled. "Let him wonder."

"Do you think that the brunette who was tracking him hit on him like you hit on me?" he joked.

She choked on her saliva, and it turned into a raging coughing fit as she tried to catch her breath. Tears streamed down her cheeks, making her embarrassment go from bad to worse.

He came over to the couch and sat down next to her and started to gently pat her on the back in order to help her clear her airway. "Jeez, I didn't mean to make you choke. I was just playing. I mean, I'm curious and all, but it's nothing worth you getting so worked up about." He let out a small giggle and she gave him a light cuff to the arm as she attempted to gain control over her breathing and clear the last bit of saliva from her throat.

"You pain in the butt. I've never hit on you," she said, her voice hoarse from her coughing fit.

He laughed. "Sure." He stretched the word like it was silly dough. He nudged her with his elbow. "It's okay if you think I'm cute. I get it all the time."

"Has anyone ever told you that you are the least humble man they have ever met?" she countered, clearing her throat one last time.

"You love it," he said, sending her a wilting smile. "Off topic, but what do you think about the brunette from the picture?"

"Chrissy?" She sighed, both relieved and annoyed they'd gone back to work instead of continuing their flirting. "What about her?"

"Is she *tenacious*?" he asked with a quirk of the brow.

"She would do whatever she needed to do to get information, but I don't think she would take a man to the bedroom that she didn't want. We're no different than men in this field."

He put up his hands in protest. "I'm sorry—I didn't mean any offense. I just wondered because Shawn was pretty quiet about her. Normally, he has opinions about all the women he has to deal with—good or bad."

"So, if he is quiet, it means that he was sleeping with her?" She gave a dry chuckle. Marie wasn't offended, not even a touch. People in their world made up their own minds about who shared their beds, and she certainly wasn't in a position in which she could judge Chrissy when she was growing dangerously close to a man she could have called her mark.

"I'm just saying there's something to the Shawn-and-Chrissy situation. I'd lay money on it," he said, winking at her.

"Is that what you guys were talking about out there?" she asked, motioning toward the window and where they had been standing outside.

"After our dressing down from Emily, we needed a little levity." He smiled. "We just got wrapped in talking about old times. You wouldn't believe half the things we've gotten ourselves into." His features flickered and a darkness seemed to cast over him. "Up until recently, it has all been pretty innocuous."

"We'll get this figured out. That's what I'm here for." She noted her phone. "And if there really is something happening between Shawn and Chrissy, perhaps I can get her up here and we can put our heads together."

"It may not be a bad idea." He dropped his hand to her knee, and the action was so smooth that it was almost natural.

His thumb moved over the clean fabric of her jeans. "You know," she started, "us working together, it probably means that we should keep things at a professional level."

She looked up from where he was touching her and caught his gaze.

The darkness had been replaced with another, more carnal, expression—one she knew well. She mirrored him, moving her gaze down to his lips and then back up to his eyes. He was so handsome.

Before she could stop him, he had his arms around her and his lips were moving against hers. He smelled of fresh air and sweat, and his kiss tasted of salt and peppermint gum.

His hand moved up her back, and he took hold of the hair at the base of her neck, gentle but firm, and he drew her mouth deeper to his until she groaned into his mouth. Her body ached for him, every inch.

It had been so long since she had been touched in such a way. His hand on her back, the welcome pain of the tug, the heat of his kiss—perfection.

Wade left her breathless as he broke the kiss and smiled at her as he released his hold on her hair and let his hand drift down to her back. "This is professional as I want to be with you."

She moved onto his lap and cupped his stubbled cheeks with her scraped hands. The pain felt so good. "You are too good looking for your own good." She kissed his lips, but he was smiling.

"I could say the same thing of you," he said, kissing her as they both let out tiny, sweet giggles.

She loved this, this feeling of stolen bliss in a treacherous world. His hands moved up her skin, and he pulled her down onto him, making her feel exactly how his body was reacting to their kisses.

Their bodies pressed against each other, moving in rhythm with their kiss.

Marie tilted her head back as his lips moved down her throat and found the V-shaped hollow at the base of her throat. He moved his hand under her shirt, thumbing her bare nipple and making it hard under his finger.

It would be so easy to take him. Here. Now.

She wanted every second of this. All.

There was a knock on the door. "You two, get your hands off each other!" Shawn yelled. "Emily wants to talk to you, Marie. You will need pants."

She hurried off Wade's lap, wiping away the lingering wetness of his kiss from her lips. "You don't think—"

"He heard us?" Wade sent her a sexy smile, his eyes were heavy with lust. "You were moaning pretty loud. Now I'm dying to hear how loud I could get you to be."

She covered her mouth with embarrassment, wishing that she had been more aware. This hadn't been the time or the place to let her guard down—no matter how badly she had wanted *that* kiss with *that* man. And oh, what a kiss it was.

Shawn knocked again. "Emily is champing at the bit. You better hurry up with the buttons, lover girl." He laughed.

"I'll be right out," she answered.

Emily could want any number of things, but if she had to guess why the woman had asked for her specifically it had to have been because of her ties to Falcon.

If things went like they had with Wade, at least with Emily she didn't have to worry about things turning toward the bedroom. She let out a giggle at the thought.

"You thinking about what I'm going to do to you later?"

She looked over her shoulder at Wade as she slipped on her boots. "We are keeping things professional, sir." She smiled, but in her heart of hearts she knew what she was saying was the truth—they needed to keep things out of the sheets.

"You say that now, but just wait until I kiss you again."

She couldn't wait, and that was the greatest problem of all. If she couldn't stop herself from falling for this man, not only was she putting herself and the investigation in danger, but she could also be putting Wade's life on the line.

Chapter Fifteen

That had taken an unexpected, but very welcome, turn. Wade stood up and undressed before jumping into the shower. It didn't take long to wash yesterday's and this morning's dirt from his skin, but as he finished, a fresh wave of tiredness washed over him.

He couldn't remember the last time he had really slept.

Grabbing some clean clothes out of his bag, he slipped them on. He picked up his phone and checked his messages as he lay down on the bed in the cubicle-sized bedroom at the end of the camper. He closed the door with his foot, blocking out some of the noise from the set as the actors and crew filtered by, talking about the rumors they were hearing on the set about the dead guy and everything else.

He tried to focus on the dozens of emails that required his attention, but after answering the most important, he found that he couldn't keep his eyes open. It only took what felt like a blink and the world faded out, even the sound disappeared into the smooth cadence of dreams—and images of Marie.

EMILY WAS STANDING by the crime scene, which was still surrounded by yellow caution tape in order to keep out any wandering strays. Her arms were crossed over her chest as she was speaking with the director and Kim, and as they spotted Shawn and Marie walking toward them, they started to make their way over as a group that far-too closely resembled a firing squad.

"Hi," Marie said, trying to control her nerves as she stood in front of the gunners with only Shawn by her side. "What's happening?"

Emily's expression was tight, and her lips were pinched like she was trying hard not to say whatever was really on her mind.

Kim stepped forward. "You and your teams promised that we would be back to filming by eight a.m. According to Shawn, here, it is your fault that we are at a standstill."

She turned toward Shawn as her jaw dropped. How in the actual hell had he come up with her to blame?

"I can assure you that I have, in no way,

stood in the way of the investigation. I'm not quite sure what *Shawn* is referring to." She tried to suppress the rage that was boiling within her.

Shawn crossed his arms over his chest. "It's okay, Marie. I told them about your investigation into James's death. How you are working with the FBI. You don't need to hide it anymore."

With his lie, some of her anger dissipated. There had to be a reason he was playing this the way he was. He would have to explain it later, but for now she would have to just play along.

"Yes," she said, clearing her throat but her voice was still a touch raspy. "I told Wade not to out me, but I'm disappointed in you, Shawn. My supervisor is going to have my butt when I get back to the field office."

"I'm sure he will," Shawn said, looking contrite. "It was just that they were going to pull out of the ranch today, until I explained that bigger fish were at play in what had happened here."

And there it was—now his motivation made sense. He was protecting the Trappers and his friend from losing the revenue from the filming. Maybe he wasn't a bad guy after all.

If Chrissy had gotten involved with him, it might not be such a bad thing—as long as they didn't get too serious.

She thought about Wade back in the trailer. If things were to get serious there, it would only end with heartbreak.

There was no way she could stay here. In fact, they could barely keep a filmmaker here and they were paying to be on the ranch.

She had a job and a world waiting for her outside of this place—a world that didn't have room for a relationship.

"If, and I mean *if*, we're going to remain on this ranch," Kim said, pulling Marie from her thoughts, "we need to know what is happening with this investigation. We can't just trust that you will be pulling out of here today. We have fallen for that promise before."

She didn't want to point out that she wasn't the one who had made those assurances, but she was in the hot seat nonetheless. "As it stands, we believe we have a line on the sniper. We are currently looking into their location."

"Do you know their identity?" Kim asked.

Anciaux nodded, but he was doing something on his phone—probably contacting his lawyers to see how they could best break their contract.

"We have video of them. So, I believe it will only be a matter of time."

"And what about this…*mess*?" Anciaux asked, finally looking up from his phone.

Her hackles rose and she looked over at Emily who appeared as though she desperately wanted to roll her eyes. "We'll be done here as soon as we can. Isn't that right, Deputy Trapper?"

Emily nodded. "As I told you before, we will release the scene as soon as we are done with our investigation. Our evidence techs are in the office, going over what they have located on the scene so far."

"And they are working with my team as well," she added, feeling silly for her interjection.

"Yes, along with the field crew from the FBI. Our joint task force is making leaps and bounds."

"When can we have the full area back for shooting?" Kim pressed.

"Look," Emily said, finally seeming to lose her temper. "There are almost ten thousand acres on this ranch. I don't understand why you are in such an uproar about the task force closing off this small section of the ranch to look into a man's *death*."

Kim sent the deputy a wicked smile. Marie could almost see the venom dripping off her canines. "We paid more than three million dollars to be here. We rented the full ranch—everything but the main house. Which, I might add, was very generous on our part. We *let you* stay in your home."

Emily's face turned red with anger, but she clenched her jaw and kept her mouth shut.

Marie stepped forward for the family. "Not everything goes our way. For all we know, this may have been caused by your company," she said, but as she spoke, she wondered if there was an element of truth to her assertion. Until now, she hadn't even considered that as an option. "Perhaps James was just at the wrong place at the wrong time and the killer was trying to make a statement about you and your company's values."

Anciaux jerked as though she had slapped him. "You don't think..."

"Right now there are any number of possibilities," Marie added with an element of menace.

"Do you have any known enemies?" Emily asked, pushing the issue. Marie noticed a slight smirk on Emily's face.

Kim touched Anciaux's arm. "They are just

trying to shift the blame. Don't play into their nonsense."

"Like Marie said, we are looking into all possible suspects," Emily said, glaring at Kim.

Marie had been on the fence before about Emily, but now there was no denying how much she liked the woman. There was nothing like a shared enemy to bond two women.

Kim turned on her heel. "Rick, let's go. I can see that we're not going to get anywhere with these two cats."

Marie snorted a laugh. She had been called a lot of names by even more people, but the fact that Kim could think she could get under her skin by calling her a cat was about the funniest thing she'd ever heard. She'd been called a helluva lot worse by a helluva lot better.

Maybe that wasn't saying a whole lot about her, but it didn't matter.

All that mattered was the fact that the director and his lackey weren't going to get away with pushing them around and bullying them into rushing an investigation just because they wanted them out of the way and pushed back into the shadows.

As she stared out in the grass where James's body had laid, she thought about the irony of the situation—here was an entire cast of characters who were trying their best to make an audience believe and *feel* for the death and mayhem taking place on the screen. And yet in reality, the people in control couldn't handle when they were presented with what they were attempting to portray.

She watched as Kim and Rick stomped away. They were talking among themselves, mumbling quietly. There was no doubt in her mind that there wasn't a positive word being uttered.

It was hardly the first time she had been hated.

As long as Wade didn't hate her, everything would be okay. That would be her breaking point. She had already come too close to losing him already. If he actually thought she was a monster, she would be forced to believe it, too.

There had been many battles in her life, and many heartbreaks, but the thought of losing Wade was a new pain—one she couldn't have seen coming and it was like nothing she had ever experienced before.

She had dated a little before and had had a few relationships—one in which she had even thought she had loved the man. Yet now that

Wade was in her life, she realized how fruitless those relationships had been. While there had been affinity and even affection, there was nothing approaching what she felt for the man whom she had just met…and just kissed.

That really had been one hell of a kiss.

She looked in the direction of his trailer. The filming was taking part over by the south end of the arena today, away from where they stood, and the camping areas were quiet thanks to everyone being in their locations for the shoot.

Emily stepped over to her after making sure that Kim and Rick were safely out of hearing range. "I know you said that you couldn't see the blonde's face from the helicopter, but are you sure that you didn't recognize anything about her—anything at all?" She had the video of the woman climbing up into the helo pulled up on her phone, and it was playing on mute.

She watched the woman's hair flap in the wind, and she tried to find anything about the woman, from her shoes to the leopard-print polish on her fingernails, that she had seen before. There was nothing.

Marie shook her head. "I'm sorry. I wish there was something. I really do."

"Do you have any inclination, any at all, that this could be the woman from your team? Did you talk to your team leader?"

She stared at Emily. The woman had to know that there was very little information that she could share—and if it was Mallory, there would be no reason for her to tell the woman the truth and throw her teammate under the bus. As much as Marie had fallen for Wade, Emily couldn't have had a clue. Even if Emily did know, she would have been foolish to think that Marie could have answered her with full and complete honesty.

"I don't know."

Emily pinched the bridge of her nose. "Would you please see what you can do to get in touch with your team members? If we can clear them, then we can look in other directions."

That was a big *if.*

If they didn't end up cleared, she would have to choose which side of the fray she would commit to.

"And about Shawn," Emily continued. "Wade seems to think that his buddy isn't involved in the shooting, but is there anything there you think would be worth looking into?" Emily asked, looking concerned.

Shawn had come out of the woodwork, but his story did make sense.

"I can dig into him a bit more, but I don't think he's hiding anything—at least not that I have picked up on." Marie shrugged. "Then again, I live in a world of some of the best covert operators in the world. We have all been trained to be able to pull off whatever needs to be done—and to do it all without being detected."

"Are you saying you think Shawn might have played a role in James's death?" Emily asked.

Marie sighed. "I'm saying that I don't know. I wish I did. I feel just as lost as you do." She ran her hand over her face. "The one thing I can say is that he is damned smart. If Shawn wanted to disappear, from what Wade has told me about him, not only does he have the knowledge but he also has the resources."

Emily nodded, but Marie could tell that she didn't like her answer.

She didn't have to. It didn't change the reality of the lack of answers they were facing.

"I think the best thing we could do is work directly with him. Have him run his facial recognition software on the video and see if he can come up with anything." She thought about Shawn and the conversation they'd had about the clip. "And if I remember right, he said something about the number on the helicopter's tail. There would have to be some kind of flight plan filed with the FAA."

"We're looking into it," Emily said, but from her tone Marie had to wonder if they had come up with nothing. "In the meantime, I'd appreciate you doing everything in your power to get in contact with your boss and see what you can learn. I'm going to release the scene of James's shooting tonight. Unfortunately, we didn't find much—and nothing that we didn't already know."

"Did you get up to the rocky point and get the spent brass we told you about?" she asked.

Emily nodded. "I have someone from my team heading up there now. They're also going to run the truck back to the ranch."

"Let me know if they can pull any prints from the brass." She looked up at the mountain where they had hiked down earlier in the day. "And who knows, maybe if you guys follow the tracks down to where she was picked up by the helo, maybe you can find something we missed?"

Chapter Sixteen

When Wade woke up, Marie was sitting outside the bedroom of the camper, working away on her computer. She was staring at the screen intently, her brows tied into a tight frown, but when she saw him step out, she closed the screen and lay her hands on the silver laptop. "I'm glad to see you got some sleep."

"Anything happen I need to know about with Emily?" he asked, wiping the sleep from his eyes as he walked to the fridge and grabbed out a bottle of water. He drank it all and threw the bottle into the recycling bin under the sink.

Marie sighed.

"That good, eh?" he asked, moving to the table and sitting down across from her.

She tapped on the computer with her fingers like she was thinking about exactly what she wanted to tell him. It didn't bode well.

"We talked about Shawn—and whether or

not he may be more involved than he is admitting."

He dropped his head. "He didn't have anything to do with it." He paused. "You know, I was thinking—there had to be three people involved, or more. They took all those trucks. They needed drivers to get them out of there."

"No," she said, opening back up her computer and tapping on a series of buttons. "The trucks were blown up not far from where the Escalade was hit. They were burned in the attack."

"Then how did they get the gold out? It's not like someone could just run in and grab all that gold and unload it while we weren't looking. There were tons to move."

She turned the computer so he could see the images she had pulled up of the burnt-out Hilux pickups. Their tailgates were open, and the beds were empty of the steel containers that they had used to initially move the bars.

"Did you see anyone move in on those trucks during the attack?" she asked.

He stared at the image. There was the first Escalade that had looked just like his sitting at the front of the line of vehicles—completely blown out.

The teams inside the SUV and the trucks

had to have still been inside at the time of the attack—he'd been right behind them in the Escalade when the first missiles hit the lead SUV and the Hilux in the front of the caravan at almost exactly the same time.

His remaining teammates had tried to divert and move around them, but as they moved, the second missile dropped from the drone high in the sky and hit the third pickup. Before he could even say anything over the radio, the next missile struck the truck in the middle that was carrying gold.

The cabs and front ends of each of the trucks were mangled where the explosions had ripped through the metal. All of the glass had blown out of the windows with the blast, and the shards that were left had melted away from the heat of the fire and were now globs of obsidian on their frames.

He had volunteered to be one of the drivers that day. He'd never been more thankful that he had been denied. Three other men hadn't been so lucky.

As it was, he wasn't sure why he had been the one left standing when the majority of teammates were now resting in the ground.

He thought about the sound of the last missile that had hit to the right of the Escalade, blowing out the tires and making the bulletproof glass flex and shatter though it had stayed in the frame. The miss had immobilized them, but it had given them time.

Shawn and James were sitting in the Escalade with him. Shawn had been in the front passenger seat, running spotter for Mark. Andrew had been sitting in the middle between him and James.

The smaller drones their enemies had used circled over the Escalade as they had rolled out of the car and jumped over the bank of the road and into the burrow pit. The secondary backup drone dropped the bomb and buzzed off into the distance.

One second later, they would have all been dead.

He couldn't even think about an SUV without seeing all their faces.

Maybe the survivor's guilt was the same for Shawn.

He couldn't, for a single second, think that Shawn had been a part of the heist. They had all meant to be killed that day. Something had gone wrong. They were supposed to have been hit with the fourth missile, but fate or luck or whatever he wanted to call it had been on their side. They had skimmed by with their lives.

Whoever had been behind the attack hadn't planned on leaving anyone alive—not even now.

The combatants they'd planted around the hit must have reported who had gotten out, but perhaps that was when they were working on getting the gold and getting out of there. They had definitely laid down some fire, but there had only been a handful of them after the lead trucks had been hit.

"Who took these pictures?" he asked, staring at the images. The trucks were still smoking and there were active flames in the Escalade he'd been inside.

"They came to us through the United Nations. They had people on the ground near where you were attacked. They came in after the bombing and recovered the bodies that they could. They then returned them to their families."

He found a small amount of comfort that they had gone so far for the contractors. More often than not, when one of them was killed they were in locations that weren't safe enough for another team to risk a life to retrieve remains. The fact that the UN believed they were in a safe enough area after the bombing came as a surprise. If it wasn't a known hot zone for insurgents, then how had they gotten so damned unlucky?

It had to have been an inside job. There had to have been someone who knew what they were moving and had the tech and the workforce to make the hit, quickly and—so they had thought—efficiently. If things had gone correctly, there would have been no real eyewitnesses, only the words of locals as to what had happened.

It would have taken the UN and their teams of investigators months to figure out what had really happened, and by then the perpetrators and the gold would have been long gone.

The thieves had thought it all through.

They had even anticipated and prepared for a bad strike—but his team had been faster.

The only people who could have had the power and the wherewithal to get together a hit like that would have been someone like his own team.

He turned the computer completely away from Marie and stared at the icons at the bottom of the screen. He was tempted to poke around on her device.

No. She hadn't been a part of the strike.

Yet just because she hadn't been a part of the hit, it didn't mean that her group hadn't.

"What group do you actually work for again?" he asked.

Their gazes met as they studied one another. She looked down at her hands and picked at the edge of her nail. "I'm with the Falcon Group. I work under a guy, last name Trixi." She took a long breath. "Are you going to run a background on me and my team?"

"What's to say I haven't already?" he said, forcing a half smile.

"You would have known who I worked for if you'd gone deep and talked to the right people. Same way I found out all I did about you."

"Your boss made you do the legwork?" he asked, a bit surprised. "You even had to get the UN images yourself?"

She shook her head. "They gave me what I needed to know, but I never walk into anything without doing my own extra level of digging."

"Did you find out anything interesting about me? Something you haven't told me?" he asked, trying to sound playful, but he wasn't sure if he was successful thanks to the nerves welling up within him.

She reached over and closed the lid of the

computer and pulled it back toward herself. Picking it up, she slipped it into her leather briefcase. "I learned enough to know that you're an honorable man."

"You learned that from a background?" he asked, surprised.

"No," she said, looking up at him as she sat the briefcase on the seat next to her. "I learned that from being here, with you."

He reached over and took her hand in his. "You don't have to tell me what I want to hear—I already think you're an amazing woman. Sugaring me up isn't required." He smiled.

She laughed as she squeezed his hand with hers. "If I was sugaring you up you would know it. Plus, I'm really not that good at lying. It took me several attempts before I could finally pass the training they made me go through on how to pass a polygraph."

"If you can't lie, what were you going to do if a combatant got their hands on you?" he asked, fearing for her as he thought about some of the interrogation techniques he had heard that were sometimes employed in order to get answers.

She looked at their entwined hands. "I was never going to be taken, not alive anyway."

He hated that this was their shared reality—death before dishonor.

"Have you heard of the Falcon Group?" she asked.

"No. Should I have?" he asked.

She shook her head. "I was just curious. There aren't many groups that work out of the US."

"You're right. I just haven't done much looking around for another job. Vaquero's kept me pretty busy."

"Kept you? Why past tense?" she asked.

"I'm not sure if I want to go back. The money is good, but it turns out the price to my soul was higher than I expected." He paused, thinking about how James's warm blood had felt on his skin. "When I got into the game, I thought I was tough, unflappable. Turns out I was wrong."

"Were those the first teammates you had lost?" she asked softly.

He shook his head. "I'd lost others. It isn't uncommon. You know how it is. We put ourselves in situations that are so risky that not even the military will send in their own. It's why they call us."

"I don't know if I've said it to you before, but I hope you know how sorry I am for your loss. I know how it is to lose teammates. It's always one hell of a wakeup call."

"I appreciate that." He nodded, but he didn't want to think about the losses he had faced in his life. If he went there, there was no stopping the downward spiral. For now, he had to concentrate on finding answers. Anything else was going to be ineffectual.

"Do you know who would have access to the information about your operational plan?"

He tried to think. Every night since the attack, he had done nothing but think about what had taken place and how they had gotten themselves pinched in that situation, but he kept coming back to one thing—they had done exactly what they were supposed to do, down to the second.

"The members of my team, the team leader and possibly the organizational leaders who were in charge of hiring us—but that isn't always the case."

"Who was your team leader?"

He didn't want to say the name, but he couldn't withhold that kind of information. "It was Shawn." His stomach sank as he said the name. "He was running everything."

"You can't continue to tell me that you think Shawn didn't have anything to do with that attack," she said, giving him a look of quiet vindication.

No matter how the cards were stacked against him, he just couldn't think his friend had been responsible for the death of their brothers in arms. Money could make people do evil things, but Shawn wasn't and had never been motivated by the all-mighty dollar.

In the sandbox, all he ever talked about was the glory of their work and his love for the adrenaline that came with the job.

Though Wade didn't know a great deal about Shawn's family, he had never gotten the impression that they were in need. They had spent so many nights bunking in the Conexes and then thousands of hours in the different convoys together. They had talked about everything from women to politics and all that lay in between. If there had been anything, anything at all for Wade to pick up on, he would have noticed.

Shawn was an honorable man.

"Even if you are in any way getting close to right, he wasn't the one who pulled the trigger." He put his hand down on the table like it was a gavel, and he ended the conversation.

Marie pulled her hand from his, making him instantly regret his adamance.

"Look," he continued, trying to soften his reaction, "if Shawn did have something to do with what happened in Iraq, then he wouldn't have done it intentionally."

"Do you think that his operational plans were compromised?"

He pointed at her with a tilt of the head. "That…that is a possibility."

"Maybe we should call Shawn and see what he has to say?"

He pulled out his phone and sent him a text. It only took a second for Shawn to respond. "I know this will surprise you," he said with a laugh, "but he found a woman, one of the actresses or something from the set, and they are out with other members of the cast and crew tonight. He invited us to meet them. You want to go?"

She sent him a wide smile. "I warn you, I can dance like nobody's business."

Chapter Seventeen

It had been forever since Marie had walked into a bar. The last time she had even been close to one was when she had strolled by the ones in the Seattle airport. It was silly, but with everything that had been going on, she looked forward to a bit of a reprieve.

It wasn't like they were going to go out and party—they still had work to do and answers to find—but for an hour or two they could make believe that they were normal people, with normal jobs, having a normal night out with friends.

She chuckled at the thought as she slipped on her tactical boots, laced them up, and pulled her jeans over the top. No matter how badly she wanted, she would never be average—in any way.

Tonight, though, she could just be one of the Montana cowgirls.

Visions of the classic movie *Road House*

came to mind. She was reminded of Dalton's quote, *Nobody ever wins a fight*.

The line hit close to home. In the case of the fights in their life, Dalton had been on point. Not one of them had walked away with a win.

For a second, she considered maybe she had gotten a win—she had met Wade. Then again, she couldn't keep him in her life. To come so close to real love and not be able to seize it was the worst kind of agony.

Her fights would leave her fated to die alone.

But not tonight.

She stepped out of the camper. Wade was leaning against one of the white ranch trucks, with their brand on the door, waiting for her. He looked so handsome. He was even wearing a white cowboy hat tonight. She didn't know where he had gotten it, but she was glad he had found it. He made it look good.

His skin was tanned from the sun, and there were twinges of red on his cheeks from the sun this morning on their hike. She wanted to kiss the sun-warmed spots.

"The women are going to be all over you tonight," she said, giggling. "I better not have to get into a fist fight with some barrel racer."

He stood up and walked over to her. "I have a feeling you would kick any other woman's ass." He put his arm around her and hugged her to him, kissing the top of her head.

If he had called her a "good girl" at that moment she would have melted into a puddle right there at his feet.

What was it about this man that made her feel like she was? When she was with him like this, everything in her world and in her heart felt lighter, even the heaviest of situations were more bearable because of his presence.

"I've seen those rodeo girls—I don't know," she said with a laugh.

"Have you met my sister Jamie yet?"

She shook her head. "No, why?"

He helped her into the pickup before climbing in on his side. "Jamie started a really cool program at the ranch, the JMac Equine Therapy. Cameron told me a bit about it. Apparently it is an equine therapy program to help people overcome trauma and loss."

"How did that get started?" she asked, looking out at the beautiful and stocky bay mare in the pasture.

"Jamie was a barrel racer. Worked the professional circuit until her boyfriend was killed in a bull-riding accident."

"Oh, that's horrible. I'm sorry to hear that," she said.

"Yeah, it was tragic. But Jamie did a great job turning it all to a positive and honoring his memory in this way. Now she is marrying a good guy, and I think he's helping her with the business side of things. I don't know how good he really is though. I haven't met him yet."

"Are they around the ranch?" she asked.

He nodded as he pulled out onto the highway and started to head toward Kalispell. "Yeah. Actually, they may be at the bar tonight. Who knows though. These things have a way of getting big at the drop of a hat."

"What do you mean?" she asked, looking at a spot in the median where it appeared as though a car had skidded through the grass at one point or another.

"It's a Montana thing. Sometimes when life gets heavy and things are out of our control, we tend to let loose. It's always been that way. I can't explain why it is, but it's like somebody ringing the dinner bell. Everyone from three counties shows up." He looked at his watch. "And it's a Saturday night, which means it's not going to be quiet." He smiled. "You may really have to go full hands with a cowgirl. If you do, though, please do it in like a swimming pool full of Jell-O. I like red."

She cuffed him on the arm playfully. "You could only be so lucky."

For the first time since she had met him, they just laughed together. The drive didn't seem to take very long, even though it had been more than a half hour to get downtown. Her foot wasn't even shaking while she had been talking to him, which was something unusual. Normally when she was riding along with anyone in a car she couldn't help her nervousness. It came as a relief that this man could have such a calming effect on her.

"What bar are we going to?"

He pulled to a stop in front of a brick building that looked like something out of the 1800s. She wouldn't have been surprised if at some point the ground floor of the building had held a bank, thanks to the bars on some of the windows.

"This place is really cool. It's called the Vault." He motioned toward the front door that was shaped like a giant circle, complete with the circular brass handle that served as the doorknob. "This place used to be one of the first national banks in the area. They moved to a larger building, probably something more secure, before I was born."

He walked around to the side of the truck

had opened her door. “Are we drinking tonight?”

She shook her head. “It’s not that I don’t want to, but my boss would have a field day if he caught me drinking on the job.”

A dark shadow washed over his features. “I don’t know how I forgot that you were being paid to run with me.”

She could tell he was trying to be jovial, but the tone of his voice didn’t match his words. If anything, he just sounded hurt.

“I would have to say that I’m actually pretty damn lucky. It’s not every woman in the world who gets to hang out with a guy and get paid by the hour and…” She covered her mouth as she laughed, hearing what she said. “I mean… not like that… I just mean—”

He started to laugh. And for once she was glad that she had made an idiot of herself. It was nice to hear him relax a little, and ohh, that laugh. She had thought his kiss was something truly amazing, but now coupled with that laugh, plus his face…well she definitely had a man beside her who was a complete package.

He opened the door of the bar for her and waved her inside. The place smelled like stale cigarette smoke from decades past, spilled beer, and a variety of men's cologne all mixing in the hot air.

It was the perfect American bar. Honky-tonk music played in the background, thanks to a live band that was on stage. The sound was a little too loud, but she tried to tell herself it was okay and not let her aversion to loud music stop her from enjoying the night. Loud noises had a way of freaking her out, but it was because of the job, and there were times in life where she just had to let that kind of thing go in order to live. Tonight was one of those times.

"You okay?" Wade asked, dropping his hand to her lower back. It was probably meant to be an act of comfort, but it made a strange heat rise up from her before going straight to her cheeks.

"Yeah," she said, almost yelling so he could hear her above the music. "Do you see Shawn anywhere?"

He glanced around the crowded room, taking advantage of his stature. "It looks like he's up at the bar. I can't promise how many drinks he is in."

"If you think I've not had to interrogate my fair share of drunk men, you'd be sorely mistaken. In fact, drunkards are my favorite kind of people to interview. There are only two kinds—the angry or the chatty. The angry ones I don't have to play nice with and the chatty ones make it easy."

She thought about the last interrogation that she had to conduct, before Wade. Her teammate, Mallory, had brought in their target—an ISIS leader—who had been purportedly had a hand in the disappearance of a French diplomat and his family.

They'd planted a prisoner in with him inside his jail cell, a man who had sold himself as a low-level gun runner who'd been caught selling guns to ISIS members. The setup had worked, and in a matter of days the leader had turned to the man and told him information relating to other crimes that they'd had no idea had occurred.

The duo had bonded to the point that they created a batch of prison-like pruno, a fermented fruit mash–based alcohol from the food they'd been given by her team. It had smelled like a fruit fly's paradise. After they'd gotten knockdown drunk, she'd had one of her underlings pull the leader out of his cell. It had only taken a couple of hours and some well-laid threats for the man to fold and give up the location of the diplomat and his family.

They had come away mostly unharmed, though upset that they had been prisoners for so long.

"Where are you at, right now?" Wade asked, pulling her from her thoughts as he handed her a Miller High Life.

She didn't want to tell him she had been thinking about the dark, dank bowels of an Afghan prison. There was no reason to go there, not when she could be here, with him, and present in the American moment.

She looked at the aluminum can he'd given her, though they had both planned not to drink. He must have thought she needed a prop. She was glad to keep her hands busy. Though she shouldn't have been, she was nervous.

"Thanks," she said, tipping the can at him before taking a long drink.

He scowled but didn't ask her again. "Get ready for the *s*-show." He took her by the hand and led her through the crowded bar. Slipping between dancing bodies and men standing and chatting with their friends and scouting women, she felt almost like a college student again. The only thing she had been missing from those days, besides her naiveté, was her sorority sweatshirt and a miniskirt to match.

Those days were so fun. She'd been in the "nerd" sorority, where partying was done, but they were usually the ones who were back at the house and tucked in their beds before 10:00 p.m. Or they would be studying away or their upcoming finals.

Needless to say, she hadn't been invited out to any of these types of nights by a man. Maybe that was why the nerves were coursing through her. It was Wade's hand and not the requirements of the night that were chipping away at her continence.

If that was what was going on, the beer hadn't been such a bad idea after all. She would, however, be keeping the number drank to one.

Shawn waved at them as they approached. "Come on over," he yelled.

The blonde beside him looked annoyed. Shawn reached over and put his hand on her knee. She shifted away from him ever so slightly on the barstool. If Shawn was serious about taking the woman home tonight, this meeting wouldn't go long.

"How's it going, brother?" Wade asked, walking up and slapping his buddy on the shoulder. He looked over at the woman. "I don't think I've seen you around the set. I'm

Wade Trapper, and you are?" he asked, not waiting for Shawn to introduce him.

"I'm Winnie. Nice to meet you," she said, a smile taking over her features as she seemed to notice exactly how handsome the cowboy in front of her really was. She shook Wade's hand for a second too long, and a surge of jealousy moved through Marie.

She stepped forward. "Hi, Shawn," she said, leaning over and laying an over-the-top kiss on Shawn's cheek.

His eyes widened with shock as he must have been trying to make sense of what had just happened and why. Admittedly, she couldn't believe she had been so bold, but if Wade thought he could just go around making her jealous without her acting up, he was dead wrong.

Wade touched her on the lower back, and Winnie gazed down at his subtle signal that they were a *thing* then rolled her eyes like a petulant teen.

That's right, barfly, back off, she thought, a wide smile moving over her face as she gazed at the woman with contempt.

Maybe Wade hadn't been so far off the mark when he had warned her against getting into a fight tonight.

"Shawn was telling me all about you. You guys are all in security?" Winnie asked, sounding syrupy.

"Yeah," Marie clipped.

"Don't you think that's a man's job?"

The woman should have quit when she was ahead.

It had always pissed her off when anyone had the gall to say something so misogynistic and maligned. It was worse when it came from a fellow woman.

"How long have you lived in Montana?" she asked, lining up her counterstrike.

"Native. I was born in Helena," the woman said proudly.

"I'm not surprised," she said, taking the swing. "If you think women should stay in the kitchen and out of male-dominated industries, I recommend that you start getting out a little more."

The woman open and closed her mouth like she was searching for breath after the blow.

Wade put his finger in the loop of Marie's pants and pulled her back from the woman like she was an ill-mannered pup on a leash.

The woman's face turned cherry red, and a thin veil of sweat broke out on her skin. "You know, it is women like you—the ones who think they are tough as nails and untouchable—that make it hard for the rest of us. Not the other way around. You are the ones who rush into burning buildings and end up getting hurt, and a man has to come in and save you." The woman sneered as she gave her a quick up-down. "You put others at risk, all because you can't admit that you have weaknesses."

Oh, she had her fair share of weaknesses. Right now, it was checking her temper with this backwoods hillbilly witch who clearly wanted to press her buttons.

Wade leaned into Marie's ear. "Do you want to dance? This is a good song," he added, like he couldn't hear the lead-up for battle with the blonde.

Marie looked at him to see if he really wanted to dance or if this was just his best attempt to get her to back down.

His breath tickled her ear. "Don't forget why we are really here."

She sucked in a breath, forcing her rage back into the ditches of her psyche.

After taking her beer from her and sitting it down on the bar next to Winnie, he held out his hand and led her toward the dance floor. The band was playing a flat version of "Friends in Low Places." To Wade's credit, it was a good song and not one she had heard in a long time.

He two-stepped around the floor with her, weaving between drunken couples, several of whom were singing with the country classic.

When they were out of earshot, he pulled her close against his chest. "Have you ever done an interrogation before?"

"What does that mean?" she countered.

"I mean you are acting like a jealous, lovestruck idiot and not the confident and professional woman I've come to know."

He wasn't wrong. She just hated that he had taken notice of her behavior and not only felt it necessary to remove her but to then chastise.

"You sit back and listen to someone who should be in your corner tell you that you are in the wrong career. Not only that, but it's not because of your ability or your aptitude but because you have the wrong set of body parts. She's lucky I didn't punch her." She looked over at the smug woman who was leaning her back against the bar, her elbow on the wooden surface behind her as she watched them dance.

Winnie was probably thinking about how Marie would have been more fit for the ballet than carrying the Sig Sauer that was strapped to her hip.

"You know what, I think I am going to punch her."

Wade hardened his grip on her hand as they danced. "You will do nothing of the sort. You are going to dance with me, and you are going to pretend to like it. Whether you do or you don't, the decision is up to you." He leaned in, close to her ear, and the stubble on his cheek grazed her face. "I, personally, am going to think about what happened back in the trailer and dream about what could have happened if we hadn't been rudely interrupted."

There was seizing the moment, but she wasn't sure that would be exactly what she would call what he had said—if anything, he was playing games with her heart. He knew just as well as she did that if they were to cross the bridge of physical intimacy, there was no going back.

Corey could call her back to the fold at any moment, especially after he had spoken to her and she had been less than forthcoming with information. She could be easily replaced.

Maybe there was something to seizing the moment and pretending the world wasn't crashing down around them and no one could really know who to trust.

She leaned into Wade, and he tightened his

hold on her back as he pressed her closer into his body. "You're not thinking about punching anyone now, are you?" he asked, the tenor of his voice vibrating against her chest thanks to their nearness.

The music filled the space between them for a moment. "I think you're safe from physical harm when it comes to me. However, I would recommend you keep me close so I can't get a full swing if I change my mind."

He laughed and the sensation against her made a strange tightness in her chest. She wasn't sure, but it felt like joy—mixed with another emotion she feared to name.

"I'll do my best. I don't need a black eye." He kissed her forehead, just above the cut on her cheek. "How is that feeling, by the way?"

In all reality, she had forgotten about the jagged rip on her face. "I'm okay. Does it make me look mean though? You know, like I could kick Winnie's butt?"

His laugh returned. "You are one helluva woman—has anyone ever told you that?"

She thought about it for a moment as they moved with the beat. His eyes found hers, and she sank into them. "You know, I don't think anyone *has* ever said anything like that to me before."

He frowned as if he didn't believe her. "There's no possible way that's true. You've had to have been told that by a thousand guys."

She waved at her ripped face and the clothes that she'd put zero thought into before going out. "Do I look like someone who gets hit on by every man who walks by?" She huffed. "That's a rhetorical question, by the way. I'm not looking for platitudes."

"You may not be looking for them, but the truth of the matter is that you are an incredibly special woman. You're unlike anyone I've ever met before, at work or in my personal life. From the moment you showed up, we clicked. You do know how rare that kind of thing is, don't you?"

She wanted to fall for his beautiful words, and as she looked at him, all she wanted to do was kiss his pouty, full lips and see if he still tasted of peppermint.

Before she could make her move, his lips found hers. The world around them disappeared, and for that brief moment in time, all that existed was Wade and his swoon-worthy kiss.

Chapter Eighteen

Though he hadn't finished his beer, Wade found that he was thoroughly intoxicated. The kiss with Marie had been even better than their shared moment in the trailer. Perhaps it was the fact that they were in public, that he was showing her off to the world as the woman who wanted him, or maybe it was just the electricity of the night and the place that had filtered into their passionate kiss, but it was damned near perfect.

The bar was full of extras who had been on set, none of whom he could name though he could recognize them in passing.

Marie had been quiet, but she hadn't let go of his hand since they had kissed, nor had she stopped smiling. That smile—she was stunningly beautiful. If she had asked him for anything in this moment, he would have obliged, unquestionably.

Shawn walked across the bar, leaving Winnie sitting at the bar while she spoke to one of the actors. He had a look of rejection plastered over his face.

"What in the hell is wrong with women?" Shawn asked, thumbing back in her direction.

Wade smirked. "You can do better."

Shawn listed to the right as he took a long drink of his beer. "You didn't hear it from me, but she is a port in the storm. It's been a long time, and I'm headed back to the sandbox any day now."

"How do you know?" Marie asked, sounding clueless.

Shawn looked at her for a long moment. "I got the email today." He took out his phone and opened up the link before handing her the device.

She scanned the message and sent Wade an *I told you so* look with a tight grip of the hand, then handed the phone back to Shawn. "You ready to head out?"

He shook his head. "But at least I have a few more days."

"You back to the same FOB?" Wade asked, not having read the email.

"Yeah, man. It's going to be strange working with a new team. I'm going to be the oldest guy there, unless you come back." He sent him a questioning look.

"We'll see."

"I'm sure you received the same contract offer." Shawn dipped his phone in his direction.

Marie jerked, like she hadn't anticipated something of the sort.

"Honestly, I've been avoiding work like the plague. I've just been focusing on helping the family at the ranch for the time being."

Shawn took another swig of beer. "Yeah, man, I hear ya. I don't know if I'd want to leave if I had a woman looking at me like Marie is looking at you, either." He laughed, sounding drunk.

"On that note," Wade said, trying to temper the blush that was rising on his cheeks, "we're going to go dance."

Shawn laughed, lifting his beer high in salute. "You're a lucky man, Wade, a damned lucky man." He swayed as he moved away, veering toward a brunette who had just walked into the bar as he called after her.

Wade led Marie back onto the dance floor, and they started to sway to the slow song that was playing, one he didn't recognize. "Did you get the answers you wanted?" he asked.

She nodded. "Why didn't you tell me that you were asked to go back into the field?"

"Honestly, I haven't even looked." He shrugged.

"You going to take the next contract?" she asked.

He had no idea what he wanted to do, but he wasn't rushing toward losing any more of his teammates or friends. He had seen enough death to last him a while.

"I don't have any plans other than being here with you right now. I'm not going to do anything until I get to the bottom of James's death. He didn't deserve to be killed as he was." He paused. "You didn't answer me about Shawn. Did you get the information you needed?"

She nodded as they danced. "If I was his captain, he would be out of a job."

"Why do you say that?"

"He may be good with technology, but he isn't great with personal privacy. He is a liability—he never should have handed me his phone. I could have access to everything from that device for the rest of the time he carried it, were I his enemy."

"So, you think he was the weak link? That whoever carried out the attack in Iraq got the information required through him?"

"Without a single doubt. They are probably still tracking his phone or his computer."

"He had been talking to James—they were planning on coming here." Wade stopped moving as the reality of the situation all came together, everything that had happened to them up to this had been well organized and planned in advance. The only wild card had been *him*.

"We have to leave. My family is never going to be safe as long as we are here. Whoever it is that is coming for you, they're never going to stop." He thought of the email. "Maybe I would be safest going back overseas. At least I'll have a full team there, a team of killers."

Marie gazed into his eyes. "Let's go back."

"Back where?" he asked, his thoughts of Iraq.

"To the camper. I don't want to dance anymore." There was a deep sadness in her voice that made him regret ever having spoken his thoughts aloud.

He waved goodbye across the bar to his brother, Cameron, and the rest of the crew from the ranch who had just made their way to the bar.

As they made their way out of the bar, he would have been lying if he had said he was disappointed she had wanted to leave. There wasn't a part of him that wanted to stay there, around so many people. All he wanted as to be alone with Marie and to spend a moment in peace before whatever war he was going to have to face.

The air was cool, and it smelled of smoke as the ash from the fires around the state settled in the valley for the night like some kind of shroud.

"Are you tired?" he asked.

She nodded. "I don't want to sleep though. I'm afraid of where my mind would go tonight."

He couldn't agree with her more. "If you're okay with it, then," he started, "what if we skipped the camper and I took you somewhere else?"

She smiled at him, but there was a tiredness that had nothing to do with sleep in her eyes.

He helped her into the truck. His thoughts were on Shawn and how he would have to go about telling his bosses at Vaquero that one of their most valuable members might have also been their biggest liability and cause for loss.

Though he didn't want to blame Shawn for the deaths that had occurred, a sensation of rage welled within him. The man should have known better. But who knew, perhaps it was just tonight that Shawn had made such a catastrophic mistake. And yet as he thought of that, he knew it wasn't the case. He'd seen Shawn drinking before. There was no doubt that given the right woman, on the right night, a spy would have had carte blanche to anything they wanted from that man and, as a result, his team.

They had been utterly betrayed by a drunkard.

What a fool.

As he climbed into the driver's side and started the pickup, Marie reached over and opened her hand, waiting for his touch. He was happy to oblige, and he was even more grateful for her not asking if he was all right. She had to have known the thoughts he was battling which all focused on the man who had been in control of so many things in his work and personal life.

They just had to find the woman with the gun. If they did, he could learn the truth and perhaps stop Shawn from costing anyone else their life.

That was to say nothing of the possibility of Shawn perhaps being a spy. If he had been so nonchalant about handing away his tech and his privacy, it could have been a clue that he didn't fear anyone because he was already playing both sides.

There were a number of possibilities, but all were disheartening.

They rode in silence, but she grazed her thumb over the back of his hand, and it brought him some comfort from his thoughts. Their bond was strange, given the circumstances which had cast them into each other's lives, but he was glad she'd been brought to him.

They pulled into the entrance of Glacier Park, and he smiled over at her. "You have to see this park at night. I used to do this in high school—it's incredible."

There was only a smattering of other cars on the road, as the majority of tourism had decreased because of the unpredictability of Montana fall weather and given the late hour. On the way up Going-to-the-Sun Road, he caught the occasional flash of glowing eyes as animals looked up and then spooked away from the side of the road.

As the neared the top of the pass, he pulled the truck over on a pullout and turned off the headlights and the engine. "Are you feeling brave?"

"Always." She squeezed his hand and then let go and turned to open her door and step out.

"Good. This is one thing that's worth all the risks. But just remember—don't run if you see a bear," he teased.

She stopped, her fingers trembling slightly on the door handle. "You don't think..."

"That there are bears out here at night?" He laughed. "I can absolutely promise you there are both black bears and grizzlies. However, they are probably going to be more afraid of you then you are of them."

"You are such a brat." She huffed.

"I just wanted to check to see how brave you are. Now I know you can stare down any enemy combatant, but you draw the line at bears."

She stuck out her tongue. "Hey, I don't see you out there trying to snuggle up to one, either."

He leaned over the console of the pickup and gently lifted her chin with his finger. "The only surly, bearlike animal I want to snuggle up to is you." He kissed her lips.

She put her hand on his chest as though she wanted to push him away, but instead her hand moved upward and she placed her hand on his cheek.

He leaned back to look her in the eyes. "You really are a cute bear."

"Watch it, sir, or I'll be the most dangerous one you'll ever come across," she teased.

He threw his head back with a laugh. "You know, I don't doubt that for a second."

Marie really was perfect.

Reaching behind him, he rummaged around in the back seat of the pickup, looking for a blanket until he came up with and red-and-blue checkered one with the ranch's brand embroidered on the corner. Pulling it out, he stuffed it under his arm. "You ready?"

"What exactly are we doing? You didn't bring me up here to just drop me off, did you?" She winked at him.

"You know, the way you keep messing with me, I just may," he teased her. "Actually…" He paused. "Now that I'm really thinking about it, why don't you just leave me here and let me run away for a while."

She shook her head. "You're not going to go anywhere without me. Not until I know you're safe. Then I'll quit bugging you."

Just like that, he was brought back to reality—she was still investigating him.

Yet for tonight, he was going to push it all to the side and concentrate on what he had planned. Nothing else had to matter for this moment.

"You couldn't bug me even if you tried. If you haven't noticed, I enjoy having you around." He stepped out of the truck, fearing that the longer he sat there the harder it would be to accept that their friendship was ill-fated.

He could feel her watching him as he walked around the front of the pickup, and she smiled as he stopped beside her door. There was a strange sadness in her eyes, and he wondered if it mirrored his own.

As he opened the door, she slipped out and moved into his arms as though there was a magnetic draw between them that could not be denied. It made him wonder if she was as in need of his touch as he was of hers.

She kicked her door shut behind her, and as their lips met the world around them disappeared and there was only them and the way her body fit against his.

He loved the way she smelled of floral shampoo and fresh air. Everything about the woman excited him, and as he moved his lips down her neck, she moaned, making his body harden with a deeper want and longing than he could ever remember feeling before. He moved his hand over her breast as he tipped her head back.

He unbuttoned her shirt slowly, taking his time as he kissed each place his fingers grazed against her skin. She tasted of sweat, but there was a natural sweetness on her skin and it made him hunger for more.

"Wade." She said his name as though it was made of honey and it was dripping from her tongue. "I want you."

He stood up and looked at her in the moonlight. She was perfection standing there. The steep glacial moraines framed her, and the stars danced in her eyes like mischievous sparks.

"You are so beautiful." He picked up the blanket he'd taken out of the pickup and walked around to the end of the pickup. Opening up the tailgate, he spread the blanket out over the cold metal.

She stepped beside him, and he turned to lift her onto the tailgate and found her naked. His breath caught in his throat. "Oh." The sound escaped him like an animalistic grunt, and it almost embarrassed him until she smiled proudly.

Instead of speaking, she reached over to him and unbuttoned his shirt and pushed it from his shoulders. She pulled it off and sat it on the tailgate. Dropping to her knees, she unbuttoned his pants. He leaned back against the tailgate, forcing himself to think about the stars and not what her hands were exploring on his body.

He had to please her, and if he was going to do that, she would need to be careful, or he would need a second chance. It had been a long time since he'd been in a situation like this, and even longer since he'd been in it with a woman he actually cared about and wanted to see again.

"Marie." He moaned her name as she took him into her mouth and flicked her tongue over his length, finding the end of him. He'd never felt anything more incredible in his life, in a more incredible place or with a more incredible woman.

It was all too perfect and almost too much as she moved her hands over him.

Reaching down, he lifted her. She wrapped her legs around him as he spun her around and put her onto the tailgate. "I don't want your knees in the dirt. You're too good for that. Besides, I haven't told you, but I'm a giver." He smirked, reaching down and finding her wetness.

He slipped his fingers inside of her, making her gasp as she stared him in the eyes.

She wanted to say something to him, he could tell. Instead she leaned in and took his lip into her mouth and sucked hard. She exhaled into his mouth, the breaths mingling into one.

He worked his thumb over her as she reached down and stroked him.

Breaking their kiss, he leaned back. “Do you want me to wear something?”

She shook her head. “I want to feel all of you.” She pulled him gently toward her.

Without removing his fingers, he led himself to her entrance, and moving his fingers out, he pressed himself into her warmth.

She gasped as she stretched around his length. He moved slowly at first, taking his time and working with her body.

Their kiss was unlike anything he had ever experienced, and he found everything he’d ever been missing in his life in that moment, and for these precious minutes, he was exactly where and with whom he was meant to be.

It could have been the sex, the moment, or the world around them—and maybe it was the conglomeration of it all as he pressed deeply into her—but he couldn’t deny to himself that he loved her.

“Wade…” she moaned. “I’m close.”

He kept his pace, moving inside her as he kissed her neck.

Her breath quickened as her body started to quake against him. She made a squeaky, choking sound. "Yes… Yes…"

Wetness spread down him, and as she finished, he couldn't stop himself.

"Marie, you're mine," he said, filling her.

She dug her nails into his skin as he drove hard into her, finding what they had both been missing.

Chapter Nineteen

The ranch was silent when Marie woke up and made her way out of the bedroom. Last night was so magical that she could hardly believe it was real. Her hand dropped to her lower belly, and the slight ache was the only way she knew for sure what they had done was real.

He was everything she had wanted in a man and everything she didn't want, all mixed into one. If she could have a real relationship and a future that wasn't just work, he would be the perfect husband. As it stood, as soon as she talked to Corey and she told him what she had found about Shawn, she would probably be back on the road after taking on another contract.

A pit formed in her stomach as she thought about leaving the magic of Montana and never seeing Wade again.

That was to say nothing about the possibility of him getting hurt. She had to find the killer and the people responsible for the missing gold.

Her phone pinged with a message from Corey asking her to call him. It was as if her just thinking about him and the things she didn't want to happen had somehow bought them to fruition.

Slipping on her boots, she stepped out of the camper, quietly closing the door behind. Corey answered on the first ring. "Where were you last night?" he asked. "I texted you several times, and you didn't respond. I was concerned."

She looked down at her phone. "I'm sorry—I didn't see your messages. Was there something you needed?"

"There was another attack on a caravan in Iraq—another shipment of gold."

A sense of relief passed through her. "So, you think it had nothing to do with Wade and his team?"

There was a long pause on the other end of the line. "Actually, that's the problem. It was still the Vaquero Group that was hit."

She sucked on her teeth thinking about Shawn and his talking about going back to the group last night. Did their being hit without him or Wade being there still clear them but implicate another member of their group?

Things were getting deeper than she had anticipated.

"Have you found anything of interest? If you haven't, I think it's time you are pulled."

"I can't leave." She sounded abrupt. "I mean, there is still a shooter out here, and I think there is still a threat to Wade and Shawn."

"Shooters aren't our problem, Marie. Do I need to remind you we're looking for answers, not on a protection operation?"

She checked her frustration. "Yes, sir. Just give me more time. I'll get our answers."

"You have twenty-four hours. Your plane ticket is in your email. If you fail to comply, you will be looking for a new company, or worse."

"But—" She started to argue, but the line went dead.

She didn't dare to consider what *or worse* meant.

Shawn was walking out up the hill from the tent camp down by the river, zipping his pants. As he spotted her, he waved. He had a mischievous grin on his face, as though he had been caught with his hand in the metaphorical cookie jar. She would have wondered what she had caught him at, but at that moment, the dark-haired woman from last night looked out of the far tent and said something she couldn't hear, making Shawn laugh.

Apparently, Marie and Wade weren't the only ones who had taken their relationship to the next level last night.

She patted her hair, thinking about how it must have looked for her to be standing outside of Wade's trailer. Shawn must have been assuming the same of her that she was assuming of him. She didn't need him thinking anything of the sort.

He hurried up the hill and made his way to her. "Ya have a good night?" he asked, pointing at the trailer as she slipped her cell phone into her pocket.

She tried to control the blush she could feel rising on her cheeks. "It was nice. We went for a drive after the bar. I see you made it back... *safely*." She nudged her chin in the direction of the extra's tent.

He laughed. "I didn't get a lot of sleep."

There was the sound of someone talking inside the barn, and Shawn pressed his fingers to his lips, telling her to be quiet.

There was a woman talking, but Marie couldn't quite hear what she was saying.

It was too early for most people to be awake, unless there were secrets at play.

Shawn took her by the hand. The action surprised her, but there was nothing other than familiarity in his touch. He pulled her around to the parking lot, following the sound of the woman's voice. There they spotted her standing behind a large maple along the dirt road, near the main ranch house,

Shawn let go of Marie's hand and motioned for her to stay back in the shadows cast by the early-morning sun rays which were just starting to crest the top of the mountains.

He slipped into the darkness of the deep shadows, moving along the walls and showing exactly why and how they had all been working in contracting. Watching him work made her want to text Wade and tell him to come.

It bothered and didn't bother her that she wanted to reach out to him. It was just new that she found it in her heart that she wanted to have him with her. She could think of no other time in her life when her first gut reaction was to call a man. Well, unless that man had been her boss and she was contractually obligated to make the phone call.

The woman kept moving as she spoke. Her

voice grew faint, but this time Marie was sure she heard her say the name "Wade."

Her heart raced.

She tried to tell herself that there were a number of reasons a woman would be talking about the handsome contractor who she had spent the night with, but she found no respite. There was something in the tone which told her that the woman was dangerous. She needed to see this woman's face to know who was speaking about the man who she cared so deeply for.

Just like that, she went from wanting Wade to be there to wanting to keep him safe and away from harm. The last thing she now wanted was for him to be there and near this dangerous woman.

Then again, maybe she was making something out of nothing. It seemed nonsensical their enemies would be so close. It would even be audacious the killer would stay on the ranch and in plain sight while hunting down one of the Trappers.

Then again, if a person did well, and did their job to the best of their abilities, they could hide anywhere. She thought of all of the women she had met since she had entered Montana and this ranch.

She thought of Emily, the sheriff's deputy.

Though she was Wade's sister-in-law, it didn't mean there was love between them. In fact, two brothers and a multimillion-dollar ranch could spell trouble. However, she had never gotten the sense Wade had been at major odds with any one of his siblings.

And Emily had no justification for shooting James, so that didn't make sense.

There had been a handful of extras and actresses—Scarlett being one of them—but there were no easy-to-spot motivations for any of them to kill.

Her thoughts moved to the director, Anciaux, and his minion, Kim Gonzalez. She would have been lying if she said she found them even the least bit endearing, but that did not equate to them being her enemy. Nor did it mean that they would have it out for James and Wade. If anything, they were the ones responsible for hiring them and paying them, so they were somewhat allies. Then again, there was the old idiom *keep your friends close but your enemies close*r.

Maybe that was the case for one of the many women she had around her—including the women from her own team.

Shawn slipped around the side of the house and out of view.

What if Shawn was the shooter? If somehow they had gotten it all wrong and read the scene incorrectly?

"Marie?" Wade called from behind her.

She turned with a start.

"How long have you been following me?" she asked.

"I heard you slip out of the camper. What are you doing?"

She motioned for him to be quiet and come closer. His hair was mussed from their activities from the night before. "Shawn is following someone." She pointed in the direction he had disappeared.

Wade rubbed the sleep from his eyes. "Why?"

"We heard a woman talking on the phone. I heard her say your name." She tried to sound unconcerned, but she wasn't sure it had worked as he looked at her.

"This can't turn into a witch hunt," he finally whispered. "If you need to go back to your group, you can go. I won't stop you. I know you have a life that doesn't revolve around me. And if you don't think you are going to find answers for your case here, then there is no real, logical reason for you to stay."

His words felt like a knife straight to her heart. "You heard my call?"

"The walls of the camper aren't that thick."

She wasn't quite sure all that he could have heard, but clearly, he had heard enough to get the gist of what was said and implied—she was staying for him. Now apparently, he didn't want her here.

"If you don't want me, we can leave last night as a flash in the pan. Or when we are in the same country and we have the chance to cross paths, perhaps we can meet up." She waved at him, trying to act as though she didn't care, even though all she wanted to do was tell him was that she wanted him to stay with her forever.

She needed him. He was her first thought and the man she wanted to call when things were in the air.

It was a new world.

Yet perhaps it wasn't such a good thing to have these kinds of feelings in her life. It was better to be alone. To love and to give her heart was to put herself at a level of vulnerability she neither wanted nor needed.

In Wade's own life, his trust of another had likely caused the death of all of his friends, though that still remained to be seen—*if* she ever found the truth.

Wade reached over and took her hand in

his, the same which Shawn had held only minutes before. “We can be whatever you want us to be, but I’m not going to stand in your way. I don’t know what I want to do with my life, and I’m not going to stand in your way.”

He wasn’t standing in her way, not in the slightest. If anything, not that she wanted to admit it, he was standing at the goal line.

She opened her mouth to speak, to tell him her truth—that just like him, she didn’t know what the future held. Yet as she was about to speak, there was the explosive sound of a shot being fired near where they stood.

“Shawn!” Wade said, his eyes widened with fear.

She reached to her hip, but she had been in such a rush to leave the camper, she hadn’t put on her Sig. All she had was the gun she carried in her boot, a small Glock 42. The weapon wasn’t known for its reliability, but it was small and good in a pinch.

Reaching down, she pulled it out of the top of her boot. Without waiting for Wade, she moved in the direction of the gunfire. There were two more shots.

Bap. Bap.

They came in rapid succession. She sped up, but Wade passed by her in a dead sprint.

She tried to catch up but found herself wanting.

They passed by the ranch house and toward the far pasture. There, standing in the backyard near a wooden playset, was Shawn. He was taking cover behind the structure, crouching down as another round whizzed through the air.

Bap.

Wood exploded in front of him, falling to the ground like confetti.

Wade pulled to a hard stop beside the edge of the house, Marie next to him. "Can you see who is shooting?"

Her first thoughts went to the sniper on the mountain. The last thing they could combat was another sniper. If they walked out in the fray without knowing where their enemy was located, they were as good as dead.

"Shawn!" Wade yelled. "Where's the shooter?"

Barely moving, Shawn pointed toward the opposite end of the house. "Stay where you are. I don't think she's alone!"

Shawn moved like he was about to stand and run toward them, but as he did, there was the crack of a shot, and he dropped to the ground.

"Shawn!" Marie screamed. She started to step toward their friend, but Wade grabbed her and thrust her against the wall next to him, hard.

"I can't lose you." Wade stared into her eyes. "You have to stay safe."

Chapter Twenty

There was nothing quite like waking up and running straight into a gunfight. Wade would have liked to say it was the first time he had experienced something to that effect, but that would have been a lie. This was hardly his first rodeo. It had just never occurred to him that he would have to fight like this on his own family's ranch.

He had his hand on Marie's back and the other on his Glock, and he had never felt anything more uncomfortable. It caught him off guard how quickly his touch could go from the tenderness of last night on the mountain to the harshness of protection in war.

And now…he had once again failed to protect another of his friends on his home field. He had lost everyone he had called a friend—everyone except her. If she thought he was going to let her walk out into the battle she was absolutely wrong. There was a greater chance of her walking on the moon.

He peered out at Shawn, hoping he would see his friend's chest rise or fall—any evidence that he was still alive. If he was just injured, there was still hope. Taking out his phone, he texted 911, letting them know there had been a shooting at the ranch and there was a man down behind the house.

The dispatcher responded back at once, but he didn't read the message and instead slipped the phone back into his pocket, finding solace in the fact that both police and EMTs would be on their way.

"Can you see who was shooting?" Marie whispered from behind him.

He shook his head. In the thing morning light, he could barely make out his friend let alone an enemy in the darkness.

He'd made a mistake talking to Shawn. Not only had he called attention to his friend's location, but he'd also let the enemy know Shawn hadn't been alone.

What an idiot. How had he been so stupid? It wasn't like he hadn't been in war, and yet he had made such a stupid mistake. Why had he been driven to such recklessness?

"We need to find the woman before she kills

someone else." Marie made to move again, reminding him about the source of his anger.

He hated it, but he couldn't deny the fact that she would get him killed if he wasn't careful. It wouldn't be her fault, but he would make a mistake and find himself in the cross fire trying to protect her—without a doubt.

"Let's get you back to the camper. We need to get our Kevlar on. No sense being out here without our gear. This shooter knows we are coming for them." He could feel the ridiculousness in his statement, but he hoped she didn't hear it in his tone.

She looked at him like he had absolutely lost his mind. "I'm not a wilted daisy. You can't treat me like I'm one."

Wade hated it, but she wasn't wrong. She was just as capable and strong as anyone who had ever been on his team, and arguably perhaps more so. Just because he wanted to protect her didn't mean he had the right to keep her tucked in the corner and out of sight.

That wasn't to say he wouldn't do everything in his power to make sure she wouldn't get hurt.

"I'm sorry," he whispered. "Let's see if we can swing around the front of the house and get the drop on our shooter. I'm sure you know but be careful if you fire your weapon. Watch what is down range—we have people and campers everywhere. I don't want anyone else getting hurt."

She answered with a tight, assertive nod. He was working with one of the best. There was no doubt about it. "How about I'll work down the front and you go out, check on Shawn, and work down the back? It's possible our shooter has bugged out. There is no reason for them to stick around. They still have the element of anonymity."

He hated the plan, but he had to agree to her line of thinking as it was the most efficient. "Okay." He stared into her eyes. "Promise me you will be safe. I can't be without you. Do you hear me?"

She stepped close and kissed him on the cheek, her lips lingering near his ear. "And I can't be without you. Don't you dare make a mistake."

The weight of her command bore down on him like stones.

The Fates must have hated him for all his life's transgressions to have put this woman in his path now, at this moment in time, when death literally stood around the corner.

"I'll meet you at the end of the house. Let's

clear the area and get this witch under control." Marie motioned toward their meeting point. "We have a life to start living—a life I want to be together."

Her candor caught him off guard.

She wanted more from him.

And he wanted all from her.

He loved her. There was no question in his heart, but this proclamation...did that mean she felt the same?

Before he could ask, she took off and moved into the morning's shadows.

If the Fates stole the woman who had become the embodiment of his heart, none would have a greater fury and no amount of justice would be enough to make up for her loss.

He simply could not live without her.

As badly as he wanted to move after her, they had made a plan, and he had promised her that he would treat her with the respect and consideration 04/28 her experience and professionalism needed.

He cleared the area before stepping out from around the corner and sprinting across the open space to where Shawn lay bleeding in the grass. As Wade neared, he could make out Shawn's closed eyes. If he hadn't seen what had happened or noticed the red splotchy liquid spilling from beneath the man's body, it would have looked as if his friend was merely sleeping.

"Shawn?" He called his name, hoping his eyes would open and he would hop up onto his elbow and make some dumb remark about bedding a woman or something true to his nature. Instead, Shawn didn't stir.

Wade drew closer and pressed his fingers against Shawn's carotid artery. His pulse was sluggish, but thankfully, it was still there and his heart was pumping away.

He pulled back up his friend's shirt. There was a gunshot wound to his left upper chest, just below his heart.

The shooter was good but thankfully not as good as needed to vanquish their enemy.

He moved to pull the shirt back down, and Shawn's hand twitched. His friend's eyes opened, and a small smile appeared on his lips as he looked up at him. "Dude, if you wanted to see me naked…" His voice was airy, and he searched hard for the next breath. "All you had to do was ask."

He laughed quietly. "You know, you're not funny, even when you're trying to kick the bucket."

"I'm…" Shawn took a breath, the sound

rattly and wet as though his chest was filling with blood due to the shredding of the projectile that had pierced through him. "I'm not kicking anything...but your ass." His eyes closed, but he tried to chuckle as he slipped back into unconsciousness.

"Help is on the way, buddy. Just hold on," he said, touching Shawn's shoulder.

He wasn't sure if his friend had heard him, but he'd like to think he had. Now, though, there wasn't anything he could do for him besides seeking vengeance for both him and his other brothers.

His thoughts moved to the moment they'd been planted in the burrow pit next to the side of the road. The last thing Mark, their teammate, had said to him was *Brothers*. As he looked out into the backyard of his familial home, he thought about the bond which came with their world.

He loved his blood brothers, but the bond he had with his battle brothers was at another level—together they had faced unimaginable loss, pain, and fear. There was no promise of permanence, no blood to tie them together—only their integrity and honor. To that end, their team's strength lay in the quality of each person's character.

There was no room for weakness or mistakes.

He glanced down at Shawn's phone. He picked it up and slipped it into his pocket. If someone was really following the device, it would bring his enemy directly to him. The chase would finally turn into a waiting game.

MARIE SLIPPED AROUND the front of the house, barely breathing as she moved out of fear that her enemy would hear her approach. She couldn't give away her position; her stealth was the only thing she had going in her favor.

Though she shouldn't have, she hated Wade wasn't beside her. She had grown accustomed to having him by her side. If she could have picked a team within the Falcon Group, he would have been her second in command. That was *if* he could take her telling him what to do.

She smiled at the thought.

In all reality, he had been so good to her. They made a great team, and his respect and adoration for her was one of the many things about the man that drew her to him.

Many in their business would have pushed her to the side in a situation like this and refused to consider anything she had said as a reasonable and logical solution for what they were facing.

Oddly enough, as she stalked through the front yard, hiding behind the bushes and moving like a cat in the shadows, she thought about the trials of Nuremberg. There, Cecelia Goetz had been the first female prosecutor. Because she had been female, she had been "too attractive" and "too emotional" to be a good lawyer. She later made history in the Krupp trial and helped solidify women's roles in not only law but male-dominated fields in geopolitics.

Though Marie doubted she would have such a visible or significant role in the world, she looked to women like Cecilia as a beacon of what was attainable, though there would always be fights to not only gain equality but keep what ground had been gained.

She hated how tenuous the ground felt, especially in less developed or very rural areas.

Coming around the potentilla bush, she brushed past the dainty yellow flowers. The morning was silent, as though no shots had been fired, and she had simply imagined that her friend was lying in the backyard possibly bleeding out on the ranch's soil.

There was a place inside her that wanted

to call out and draw the shooter's fire just so that she could find her and there would be no more concern for Wade's safety.

Anything could have happened to him, and they weren't together. An ache formed in her gut as she thought about the last time she had been forced to noiselessly vanquish a woman in Pakistan with nothing more than a shoelace.

Many things could happen in utter silence. Countries could split, gold could disappear, and lives could evaporate. In her case, love could blossom and just as quickly die.

She couldn't allow that to happen. No matter what she had to do or who she had to vanquish, she had to save Wade and keep him in her life.

There was the thrumming of helicopter blades in the distance.

No.

The shooter couldn't disappear once again. They couldn't let her get away with her crimes. Not like this. Not after what she had done to Shawn and James.

She had to be stopped.

Though Marie was aware of the danger, she ran toward the sound of the helicopter. The shooter had to be doing the same.

She needed her shot.

The only Vaquero member left was Wade, and this woman seemed hell-bent on killing each of them. That meant only one thing—it was the blonde or Wade.

If it came down to a shoelace, she wouldn't be afraid to do what had to be done to save and protect the man she loved.

The thumping grew louder, the cut of the blade drawing near.

She ran past the end of the house, hoping the blonde would be standing there, peering up at the sky. Instead, she found Anciaux talking animatedly with Kim.

The man looked furious.

She couldn't stand the duo under normal circumstances, and they were the last people she wanted to see in a moment like this.

Reaching down, she stuffed her Glock into the back of the waistband of her pants. She didn't want them asking her questions or drawing her away from her mission.

Though they might have been the ones behind her hiring on paper, her loyalties lay with…

She paused.

That was a huge question.

Until now, she had been able to answer that

question without hesitation—her loyalties had first and foremost been to her employers at Falcon. Yet now she leaned toward Wade.

That had to be love.

As much as she wanted to refuse the feeling and tell herself it was nothing more than a resonance of like-minded people with similar backgrounds, it was something much deeper and more profound. Yes, they were alike and yes there were similarities in their past, but there was something far more like kismet which had brought them together.

It was almost as if the Fates or magic or the ghost of Christmas past—whatever a person wanted to call it—had brought them together.

There was an undeniableness to their connection.

"Marie?" Kim called her.

She wanted to pretend as though she hadn't heard the woman say her name and just go back to listening for the helicopter in the distance.

"Oy, Marie!" Kim called again, refusing to ignore her.

"Oh, hi," Marie said, wishing that any moment Wade would come around a corner and appear to rescue her from the insipid woman.

"You're up early," Anciaux said, motioning for her to come closer.

She faked a smile. "No rest for the weary."

"Did you hear that loud bang?" Kim asked, pointing in the direction from which she had just come.

"Oh, that..." Marie wasn't exactly sure what to say or if she should or shouldn't admit to what she had just bore witness.

"Do you know what happened?" Kim asked, waving her hand nonchalantly.

She didn't know what to say.

"Your team promised me no more interruptions," Anciaux added, sounding angry.

Though it took every ounce of her willpower to resist, Marie held back from punching the man right in the mouth. She couldn't stand how little value the man placed in human life. While she was paid to remove the cancer from civilization and keep her targets safe, she wasn't without empathy or understanding that with every trigger pull came a snowball effect to families and loved ones. Life and death did not come lightly, but it did come.

She was the purveyor of justice, nothing more and nothing less—lest nothing and no one get in her way.

"We can't control life. All we can do is make the best of the events and conditions in which we are presented with," Marie said, trying to sound magnanimous in the face of a soulless ape.

"We can't lose another dime." Anciaux made a clicking sound.

She wanted to say something, to tell the man what she truly felt about him and his apathy, yet she had bigger battles. "Money is replaceable. Use the story of your filming to sell your show. There's no such thing as bad press." She forced a nod. "I need to go." She pointed toward the sky and the noise. She turned her back to the duo.

"Whatever do you mean?" Kim asked. "You don't need to go anywhere."

There was a maleficence in the woman's voice which made Marie turn. "What?"

As she turned to face the woman, the morning sun shone off the barrel of the woman's derringer. It was a tiny pistol, but it made Marie regret ever having put her gun away.

"Where is Wade?" Kim asked, any faux felicities in her tone disappearing.

She resisted the urge to look toward the back of the house where he was supposed to appear at any moment. She couldn't give away his position, both of their lives potentially depended on her ability to lie. “He’s in bed in the camper.” She motioned toward the camper area. “What do you want with him?”

“Don’t lie to me—I heard him yelling.” Kim countered, motioning in the direction from which they had come. “If either one of you thinks he can just pop his head up, you will be the one I will take out first.”

Marie let her gaze drift back to the gun. “That gun only has one shot. I hope you’re a good shot, because if you miss… I will kill you.”

Kim smirked. “You have a high opinion of yourself if you think you can get the drop on me. I’ve been at this game far longer than you.”

“What game as that?”

“The game of life or death. And as I hope you know, there is no room for mistakes.”

Anciaux puffed up as he raised a brow.

There was a thin sheen of sweat on the man’s nose. He could pretend he was brave and that they were in the point position all they wanted, but his body gave away his nervousness.

“Rick,” Marie started, “do you know who the woman at your side truly is?”

He smirked. "Do you?"

Marie staggered back a step.

"I didn't think so," Anciaux said with a slight British accent she hadn't really noticed before, his evil smile widening. "Just like you, we're looking for what was taken. We're just better than you. We let no one and nothing get in our way." He gave her a quick up-and-down. "And we certainly don't let sex stop us from doing our jobs from the best of our abilities."

Sex. Was the man losing his mind? Did he really think he could talk to her like that without any repercussions?

"You have me all wrong. And besides, didn't you hear?" Marie bluffed. "We've already found the missing gold. Which group are you working for?"

Anciaux shot Kim a look as though they were trying to decide whether or not she was bluffing or telling the truth. Kim shook her head almost imperceptibly.

"I already know you work for the British government and who sent you. Do you really think my bosses would really let me walk into a war blind?" Marie bluffed, trying to sell her lie to the best of her abilities.

"You are full of nothing but lies," Kim hissed, her English accent rearing.

Marie had many friends from the UK, but enemies came from every corner of the globe—even potentially from fellow Americans if they were given the right opportunity and a motivational amount of money.

"Do you really want to point fingers?" she asked. "Why did you shoot Shawn? James? Were you afraid the truth would come out?"

Kim moved closer, jabbing the gun into her ribs. "You are talking out of your hat. If you knew anything, you would have killed them and your little boyfriend long before I got the chance."

The whirring of the helo grew closer.

Was she implying the Vaquero Group had been behind the gold heist the entire time?

"Wade and his teammates didn't take the gold," Marie argued.

Anciaux laughed. "Of course they didn't, you daft woman." He looked at her like she had grown a third arm. "Their group was far too noble to do what needed to truly be done."

Kim pushed the gun harder into her ribs, right beneath the area of her heart. "Didn't your boyfriend or your bosses at the Falcon Group tell you who they were moving the gold from? Or where the gold had originated from?"

While she had done her research, those kinds of details had fallen into the category of *classified* and far above her pay grade.

She shook her head, afraid that with her admission she would invite the pull of the trigger.

"Your boyfriend was moving gold to fund a terrorist sect with ties to an underground extremist group. They stole the money from the families they eradicated in the Afghan and Pakistan hillsides."

The woman's words rang false. She'd worked in many hillside villages, and while there were certain areas with abundant resources and access to gold and silver, most didn't have the volume of revenue they had been moving.

No matter what she thought, she wasn't going to argue with the woman holding the gun in her ribs.

Marie shifted her weight away from the pistol, moving slightly as Kim looked toward the sound of the helo in the sky.

"Is that your flight?" Marie asked, reaching behind her back and putting her hand on the rough grip of her Glock.

Kim shook her head. "Actually, it's yours."

"What?" she asked, panicking.

"My Thundercloud team was hired by

the Department of Defense in the UK. We worked with the Vaqueros until they decided to go against our wishes." Anciaux sucked his teeth, and he dabbed at the sweat on his forehead. "Some members of the group knew of our plans to acquire the gold—some of which was to go to our government—while they also turned a blind eye for the team to take half in payment."

"Our mission was to be completed with no witnesses and no foreign governments to know what we had done." Kim sighed. "Unfortunately, we had to tie up some *loose ends*." She shrugged as if lives lost were nothing.

"You were the woman? The sniper on the mountain?" Marie asked, shocked by the woman's admission.

Kim's lips turned into an evil smile. "Yes. And now Wade knows he is looking for a blonde shooter. We heard all about it from the deputy. We have to give him one—he needs his justice."

Anciaux moved to grab Marie by the arm, but as he moved toward her, she stepped back and pulled the gun free of her waistband. She pointed it at Kim's center mass. "Don't you dare move," she said to Anciaux. "The police are on their way."

Kim finger twitched on her derringer, and the gun flashed.

It was strange. The noise came after the warmth in her chest. Or had the sensations come together? She moved her hand to feel the ache in her side where the round had struck and now burned like fire.

Warm, sticky blood coated her fingertips, but she didn't dare to look away.

Kim dropped to her knees as if in supplication before her. The gun in her hand skittered to the ground, landing in the dirt. There were red droplets of blood on the barrel.

The woman before her held her chest and looked up at her with terror and pain in her eyes. "How dare you..." She fell forward, landing on top of her gun.

Marie glanced down at the gun in her hand; her finger wasn't even on the trigger.

Anciaux lunged toward Marie, pulling a gun from behind him she hadn't seen. Her fingers moved downward, and she pressed the trigger, the bullet ripping out of the muzzle and piercing the porcupine-like man.

"You have no idea what you've done."

The burst of flame from the muzzle was blue as he pulled the trigger, barely visible if time hadn't slowed and she hadn't been staring at the gun in hopes it was never going to be fired.

There was only the heat of the first round, no searing pain of another hit.

He couldn't have missed her, they were too close.

As Anciaux stumbled, blood poured from his chest, and he moved to Kim's side and dropped to his knees beside her. "They won't win."

"Marie?" Wade called, rushing to her side. He held his pistol pointed at Anciaux, ready to fire again.

She turned. There was a vague sense of relief, but the numbness of shock kept her from anything more—it was all too surreal.

She lifted her hands, showing him the blood on her fingertips.

"Oh." He stared at her fingers, and his gaze dropped down to the bloody hole in her shirt where Kim's bullet had ripped through her. "You're going to be okay. I promise." His voice calm, but she could still pick up the traces of panic in the way he was almost too calm.

Perhaps he had just dissociated as much as she had.

He lifted her shirt, assessing her wound, keeping the gun on their enemy.

Anciaux trembled as he looked up. "You are fools if you think you can kill us and stop our team from hunting you down. More are coming." He pointed toward the sky as the helicopter moved in over their heads.

Wade took her hand, leaving Kim and Anciaux there on the ground, and pulled her toward the cover. He ran toward the parking area and pushed her down, pointing to the ground. "Get under the truck!"

There was the sound of machine gunfire as she slipped under the pickup. Gravel pressed into her knees and the sticky palm of her hand as she lay down. "Wade, get down!" she yelled at him.

He moved away from her, and she watched his feet as he stepped toward the front of the vehicle. "Wade!" she called after him again as another string of rounds rained down from the sky.

Strangely, there were no bursts of dust around the pickup as she would have expected.

Where were the gunners on board shooting?

There was the sound of sirens nearing the ranch.

They weren't on their own.

Wade leaned down. "Babe, babe…you have

to see this," he said, holding out his hand and motioning for her.

She was confused. Why would he want her to come out where they were actively shooting?

She crawled forward, her gun still in her hand.

As she moved out from under the truck, she looked up at the helicopter in the sky. There, flying over them, was a blue helo with Emily looking out of the door and waving down to them. She gave them a thumbs-up.

Anciaux was lying down on the ground beside Kim, his gun tossed to the side and his hands were behind his head as though he was merely waiting for jail. There were pock marks in the ground around the duo where Emily must have corralled them with her rounds.

Their enemies had been neutralized, but as she stared up at the sky, a profound sadness welled within her—her job here was done and she would be leaving.

The fantasy she had created with Wade was officially over.

The Trappers had come together to crush their enemies—but in doing what they had all been working to accomplish, her heart was going to fall into the category of *collateral damage*.

Chapter Twenty-One

The next day, Emily was the official hero, having cleared them of any wrongdoing in the shooting and handling the potential local fallout from their actions. Wade couldn't have been more grateful when she walked up onto the stage at the official press conference for the events that had taken place on the ranch. She gave him a tilt of the head and looked to Marie, who was healing well after getting a few stitches for the small-caliber wound that had pierced her side.

Thankfully, the wound had been superficial, only piercing skin and muscle, but had the shot been slightly higher, it could have been deadly.

He shuddered at the thought of the difference a millimeter one way or another could make.

If Marie had been taken from him, he didn't know how he could have recovered.

Shawn was sitting on the opposite side of the tent that the police's information officer had set up for the event in hopes of quelling public curiosity and concern.

Wade's phone buzzed in his pocket. He pulled it out and glanced at the name—Falcon Group.

He moved the phone for Marie to see. "Do you know what this is about?"

She glanced at the phone, and her face blanched. "We need to talk."

His stomach sank somewhere between his knees. That was never a good collection of words for anyone to hear—and especially not when he felt as he did toward Marie.

It blew him away how quickly he could go from being comfortable on his own with only his teammates from Vaquero to now—where he was at a loss about his future and all he wanted was to love Marie for the rest of his life.

Though he knew he should have stayed in the tent to support Emily, he clicked off his phone and took Marie by the hand a led her outside the public information officer's tent.

She walked a step behind him, looking back at the tent as though she wished she was still safely tucked inside.

Her look broke his heart.

The river was just down the hill from where they stood at the center of the ranch. In an attempt to gain control over his thoughts and feelings and what he wanted to do, he slowly picked his way down the hill.

No one could hear what he needed to ask her about work. If she was going to go back to contracting, she would need to have some level of anonymity, and he couldn't stand in her way.

According to what she had told him, her bosses had sent another team after the Thundercloud Group, who were based out of London, and they'd worked with a team of accountants who planned on recovering as much of the gold as was possible. However, little could be done to return the gold to the rightful owners.

Though he had asked his boss at Vaquero, they wouldn't tell him where the gold had originated. It hadn't sat well, but it did answer one question he'd been asking himself—he would not go back to Vaquero.

There was nothing there for him there, and he would forever struggle with the fact the group had been responsible for his brothers-in-arms' deaths. Wade hated the fact he'd had a hand in what could have been seen as less than honorable. He'd waged a war for these people. They had required integrity—and yet they had been unwilling to prove their own when it had come down to it.

Money and politics, mixed with the need for his former group's need to save face, ended up being more important than the people who were willing to lay down their lives under their flag.

His brothers in Vaquero were who had been his family—not Vaquero itself.

He sighed as he tried to quell the sting of the realization moved through him. This would all be a good thing.

It was time for a change.

It was time to embrace life.

"You okay with the walk?" he asked, motioning toward Marie's injured side.

She nodded, but her face was contorted into a look of concern.

"If you want to go back to Falcon, I won't stand in your way." He motioned toward his phone. "I'm sure they want you to head out as quickly as possible. I know Shawn is going to take the new contract. I'm sure you're champing at the bit, too." He tried to sound like he really meant what he was saying, but as he looked into her beautiful blue eyes, all he could think about was how badly he wanted to simply pull her into his arms and ask her to stay.

Yet what could he offer her? This ranch wasn't his, he no longer had a job, and his past and present was filled with more baggage than the Atlanta airport.

"What?" She sounded shocked and, though he wasn't entirely sure he was right, a touch hurt. "Are you kidding me? I'm not in a hurry. I don't want to leave you, Wade. If anything, I'm just..." She looked away from him as though she was afraid to say what she was thinking straight to his face. "I guess I'm sad."

"Hold on..." He couldn't help the smile that overtook his face. "Who said you had to leave me?"

She motioned toward his phone. "Corey did... You were right—my group wants me back. They have a new job for me, but I told him I'd only take it on one condition. Which was why I wanted to talk to you."

So, she was planning to return to contracting. The relief that had started to take over was just as quickly erased.

"What was the condition?"

She shuffled her feet. "Listen, you don't have to do anything you don't want to. I know you've been through a lot, and you may want to go back to Vaquero or stay here on the ranch with your family." Finally, she looked up at him and there was pain and longing in her eyes. "But Wade, I want you to join Falcon with me. I'm not ready to stop fighting for what is right, and I think you're not, either. I—"

He stopped her with a kiss, soft and tender—a kiss built on unspoken promises. "You're right—I'm not done. But I am done contracting for people I don't trust. I don't want to ever have a chance of losing you. I've lost so many already."

She looked surprised. "Seriously? You don't want to contract?"

He paused. "It's not that I fear fighting for what I believe in."

"What do you believe in, Wade?" she asked, taking his other hand in hers and facing him head on.

"I believe in you." He lifted their joined hands. "I believe in our love. I love you, Marie. And I don't want to have a hand in another person on this planet losing what we have."

"I love you, too, Wade." There was a stressed edge in her voice that made him question whether or not his love would be enough. "What if we started something new?" she asked.

He hadn't considered anything like that—he'd only ever been good at being a runner and gunner. What she was talking about would take all kinds of backing and political maneuvering. Was it even possible?

"What do you have in mind?"

She smiled. "That was my condition with Falcon. If I return to work, I take on an ownership chair—along with *you.* I told Corey that I want to have a group that focuses on humanitarian solutions."

"How did you think about this?" he asked, shocked and so deeply proud of her that he felt humbled by her presence.

"Corey and I were talking about the gold. I know it probably won't surprise you, but the gold actually came to Iraq from the United Nations to help fund a group who was building schools for women and girls throughout the Middle East. They are going to be kept near or on the embassies so women can study without fear of harassment or worse."

"So, we were on the right side of the gun?" he asked, wanting to sink to his knees with relief. Finally, he could sleep at night.

She nodded. "You were going to make a difference for hundreds of thousands of women and their children." She wrapped her arms around him. "Your brothers at Vaquero didn't die for nothing. About three-quarters of the missing gold has been recovered and is going to be used for its intended purpose. The United Nations has also found funding to get the remainder of the amount needed for the project."

"What about the rest of the gold?" he asked.

She motioned toward the ranch. "It sounds like it went here, to this film production. They had made a point of being on this ranch in the event. It sounded like Corey and my IT team found evidence that they had plans to kill everyone in your family, if we hadn't acted fast."

His heart thrashed in his chest as he thought about how close he had been to not coming home and then of running away once he had gotten there.

Yet they had needed his protection—albeit from a situation he had helped to create.

He would have to do something to make up for all the harm and evil he'd allowed to enter the family's lives.

"It's not your fault," Marie said, almost as though she could read his mind. "You didn't know they would sink so low. Your family is safe, and I promise—from what I've seen, if any family can handle themselves it is the Trappers."

He laughed at the thought. They were one heck of a family. Through thick and thin, they came out the other side stronger.

"Besides, now we know the ranch can be financially solvent for years to come." She put her head on his chest. "We made this place better. We helped people who needed it. Now we can move to do more. We can make the world a better place."

"I agree to your terms. I'll come to Falcon," he said, "but I have a condition of my own."

She stepped back, looking up at him, but he refused to let her move out of his arms as he smiled down at her. "If we're going to conquer the world, we have to do it as husband and wife. I want to have you with me until the end of time."

"Hmm," she said, smiling widely. "That's one heck of a condition to just throw at a woman out of left field."

"I know what I want. I'm not going to wait around to ask to get it," he said, leaning down and kissing her on the forehead. He dropped to his knee. "However, if you need me to bow to you, I will. You are the only one I would do this for, I hope you know." He smiled up at her with a cheeky grin. "Marie Costa, will you marry me?"

"Of course." She nodded, her smile matching his own. "But leave it to you to tease me even when asking me the most serious question of my life."

He shook his head as he stayed down on his knee. "If you want, I can ask again," he teased. "I'll do whatever it takes to be your husband."

She giggled, the sound so sweet and loving that just when he thought he couldn't be more filled with love, more love flowed in. "I love you, Wade Trapper. And I want you to know there is nothing that would stop me from becoming your wife."

"You know…" He pointed up at the main house. "I think Emily may know a judge or two. If you don't want a big thing, we can do it here…as soon as we can get the paperwork."

She bounced from one foot to the other with excitement. "Yes, Wade. Yes."

In that moment, as he stared up at the woman who had promised to become his wife, he was overcome with so many emotions. His thoughts went back to his friends and the family he had lost.

It was times like these, when love and honor came together to create hope, that were some of the most important things in life. Hate could be vanquished, wrongs could by turned right, and love could conquer the world.

* * * * *